# PEOPLE YOU SHOULD KNOW

# TOP 101 AUTHORS

Edited by Nicholas Faulkner

Britannica Educational Publishing
IN ASSOCIATION WITH
ROSEN
EDUCATIONAL SERVICES

Published in 2017 by Britannica Educational Publishing (a trademark of Encyclopædia Britannica, Inc.) in association with The Rosen Publishing Group, Inc.
29 East 21st Street, New York, NY 10010



Distributed exclusively by Rosen Publishing.
To see additional Britannica Educational Publishing titles, go to rosenpublishing.com.

First Edition

**Britannica Educational Publishing**
J.E. Luebering: Director, Core Reference Group
Anthony L. Green: Editor, Compton's by Britannica

**Rosen Publishing**
Nicholas Faulkner: Editor
Nelson Sá: Art Director
Brian Garvey: Designer
Cindy Reiman: Photography Manager
Karen Huang: Photo Researcher
Introduction and supplementary material by Nicki Peter Petrikowski

Library of Congress Cataloging-in-Publication Data

Names: Faulkner, Nicholas, editor.
Title: 101 authors / edited by Nicholas Faulkner.
Other titles: One hundred and one authors
Description: First edition. | New York : Britannica Educational Publishing in association with Rosen Educational Services, 2017. | Series: People you should know | Includes bibliographical references and index.
Identifiers: LCCN 2015051441 | ISBN 9781680485066 (library bound : alk. paper)
Subjects: LCSH: Authors--Biography--Juvenile literature. | Literature--History and criticism--Juvenile literature.
Classification: LCC PN451 .A18 2016 | DDC 809--dc23
LC record available at http://lccn.loc.gov/2015051441

*Manufactured in China*

Cover (top left), pp. 90, 118, 149 © AP Images; cover (top center left), p. 113 U.S. Signal Corps./National Archives, Washington, D.C.; cover (top center right) p. 57 Public Domain; cover (top right), p. 158 New York World-Telegram & Sun Collection/Library of Congress, Washington, D.C. (neg. no. LC-USZ62-111438); cover (bottom left) pp. 8, 38, 99, 127 Photos.com/Thinkstock; cover (bottom center left), p. 49 Universal Images Group/Getty Images; cover (bottom center right), p. 28 Bachrach/Archive Photos/Getty Images; cover (bottom right), p. 147 George De Sota/Getty Images/Thinkstock; p. 1 Courtesy of Louisa May Alcott Memorial Association; p. 3 PRNewsFoto/XM Satellite Radio/AP Images; p. 5 Macmillan Publishers; 44 Amherst College Archives & Special Collections (Public Domain); p. 46 Jason Kempin/Getty Images; p. 61 © Lufti Ozkak; p. 63 Courtesy of the Bayerische Staatsgemäldesammlungen, Münich, Neue Pinakothek; p. 83 Mark Mainz/Getty Images/Thinkstock; p. 101 David Levenson/Getty Images Entertainment/Getty Images; p. 107 Jeremy Sutton-Hibbert/Getty Images Entertainment/Getty Images; p. 109 Library of Congress, Washington, D.C. (neg. no. LC USZ 62 108013); p. 121 Ben Pruchnie/Getty Images/Thinkstock; p. 123 Cate Gillon/Getty Images/Thinkstock; p. 131 Courtesy of the National Portrait Gallery, London; p. 143 Mario Tama/Getty Images/Thinkstock; 151 Culture Club/Hulton Archive/Getty Images; p. 153 Darren McCollester/Getty Images/Thinkstock; cover and interior pages border image © iStockphoto.com/urbancow

# CONTENTS

28

38

101

121

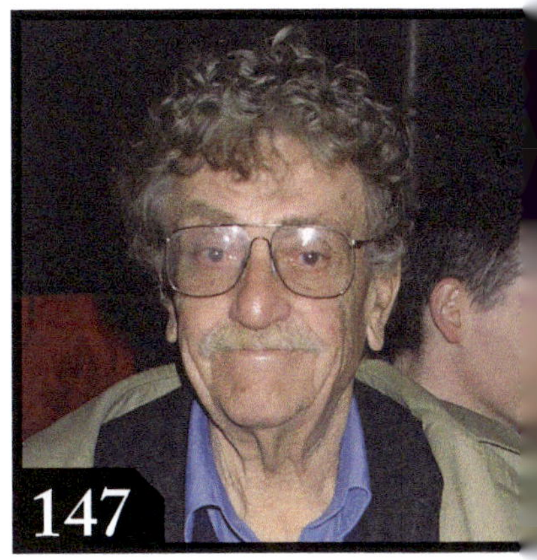
147

157

# INTRODUCTION

Writing is one of humanity's most important inventions. People have probably told stories and shared their experiences since the first words were uttered, but those tales are lost to us. Being able to preserve and disseminate information in written form has allowed us to continuously build on the knowledge of our ancestors and benefit from the efforts of past generations. And while a narrated story only reached a small number of listeners, progress in technology and education has allowed written stories to reach a much bigger audience. Some stories are quickly forgotten, whereas others captivate millions and are held in high regard for a long time, sometimes even centuries.

*People You Should Know: 101 Authors* collects the biographies of some of the best and most successful writers in history. Miguel de Cervantes, William Shakespeare, Johann Wolfgang von Goethe--the works of these writers are considered to be timeless classics, and the way they explore the human condition makes them as fascinating today as they were when they were written.

With countless genres, themes, and styles to explore, literature can always stay fresh. Authors have strived for realism in their work, minutely describing certain aspects of society, be it the village life of mid-19th century France in Gustave Flaubert's *Madame Bovary*, the descent of *Maggie: A Girl of the Streets* by Stephen Crane, or the struggles of the poor and the wealthy in the works of John Steinbeck.

Writers are not restricted to stories set in the real world, though, and they often create their own. Influenced by Norse mythology and other legends, J.R.R. Tolkien created a mythology of his own, conceiving a whole world and its inhabitants, their history, and their languages. Generations of readers have relished their excursions to Middle Earth, just as millions of children have happily visited Narnia, a creation of Tolkien's friend C.S. Lewis. J.K. Rowling's series was so popular that even people who did not read fiction otherwise picked up her books to get to know about Harry Potter's adventures in the wondrous world of wizards.

Although fantasy literature is occasionally criticized for being escapist, contrasting the real world with a fictional one can be thought-provoking and rewarding. In *Gulliver's Travels*, Jonathan Swift lets his protagonist visit fantastic lands, the curious inhabitants of which serve as a satire of the human race, and the dystopian tales told by George Orwell and Aldous Huxley ring depressingly true.

Sometimes the ideas of an author even seem to have prophetic qualities, as was the case with Jules Verne. Several of the concepts described in his books, which must have seemed unrealistic at the time, have since become a regular part of our lives. It remains to be seen if the science fiction of Isaac Asimov, who also was a prolific writer of nonfiction, has anticipated things to come.

Be that as it may, one safe prediction is that the works of the authors presented here will continue to captivate their readers.

# LOUISA MAY ALCOTT

(b. 1832—d. 1888)

Based on Louisa May Alcott's recollections of her own childhood, *Little Women* describes the domestic adventures of a New England family of modest means but optimistic outlook. An immediate success when Alcott published it in 1868, the novel remains a classic of children's literature. Alcott wrote during a period of great American literary creativity known as the American Renaissance, and she was influenced in her writing by Transcendentalist ideas. Her father, Amos Bronson Alcott, was a teacher, social reformer, and Transcendental philosopher as well as a close friend of Ralph Waldo Emerson's.

Louisa May Alcott, portrait by George Healy.

Louisa May Alcott was born in Germantown, Pennsylvania, on November 29, 1832. She grew up in Boston and Concord, Massachusetts, in the company of Emerson, Henry David Thoreau, and Theodore Parker, a Unitarian preacher and abolitionist. The Alcott family was always poor or in debt, until Louisa became a successful writer as an adult and supported the family. While she was a child, her father established a series of schools for children. His "conversational" method of teaching was far in advance of his time and won him few pupils. It was, however, very successful with Louisa. She began to write poems and stories, and by age 15 she was writing and producing amateur theatricals. Alcott published some of her stories under the name A.M. Barnard; these lurid and violent thrillers were unusual in their depictions of women as strong, self-reliant, and imaginative. By 1860 her verses and stories were appearing in the *Atlantic Monthly*.

In 1862, during the American Civil War, Louisa Alcott served as a nurse in the Union Army hospital at Georgetown—now part of Washington, D.C. She contracted typhoid from unsanitary hospital conditions and was sent home. She was never completely well again. Her letters home telling of her hospital experiences were published in 1863 under the title *Hospital Sketches* and brought her $2,000. With this money she made her first trip to Europe.

On her return home, Alcott began *Little Women*, a realistic but wholesome picture of family life with which younger readers could easily identify. The book made her famous and enabled her to pay off all the family debts. In 1870 Alcott took a long tour of Europe with her sister May. In Rome, Italy, she wrote *Little Men* (1871).

Alcott's other works include *An Old-Fashioned Girl* (1870), *Eight Cousins* (1875), *Under the Lilacs* (1878), and *Jo's Boys* (1886). The publication of some of her lesser-known works late in the 20th century aroused renewed critical interest in her adult fiction, such as the Gothic novels *A Modern Mephistopheles* (1877; republished 1987) and *A Long Fatal Love Chase* (first published 1995).

Alcott took an active part in the temperance and woman's suffrage movements. She never married. She died in Boston on March 6, 1888, two days after her father. Orchard House, in Concord, where she wrote *Little Women*, was made a memorial in 1911.

## MAYA ANGELOU

(b. 1928—d. 2014)

American poet, playwright, and performer Maya Angelou produced several autobiographies that explore the themes of economic, racial, and sexual oppression. She became the first African American woman to

Maya Angelou, 1996.

have a feature film adapted from one of her own stories when her screenplay *Georgia, Georgia* was produced in 1972.

Born Marguerite Johnson on April 4, 1928, in St. Louis, Missouri, Angelou spent much of her childhood living with her paternal grandmother in rural Stamps, Arkansas. After her mother's boyfriend raped her when she was eight years old, she went through a long period of muteness. This early life is the focus of Angelou's first autobiographical work, *I Know Why the Caged Bird Sings* (1970). Subsequent volumes of autobiography include *Gather Together in My Name* (1974), *Singin' and Swingin' and Gettin' Merry Like Christmas* (1976), *The Heart of a Woman* (1981), *All God's Children Need Traveling Shoes* (1986), *A Song Flung Up to Heaven* (2002), and *Mom & Me & Mom* (2013).

In 1940 Angelou moved with her mother to San Francisco, California. At one point she worked as a dancer, during which time she assumed her professional name. In the late 1950s Angelou settled in New York, New York, and was encouraged to write by members of the Harlem Writers' Guild. During the same time, she won a role in a production of George Gershwin's *Porgy and Bess*, and she stayed with the troupe, ultimately touring 22 countries in Europe and Africa. She also studied dance with Martha Graham and Pearl Primus. In 1961 Angelou performed in Jean Genet's *The Blacks*. That same year, a South African dissident to whom Angelou was briefly married persuaded her to move to Cairo, Egypt, where she worked for the *Arab Observer*. She later moved to Ghana and worked on the *African Review*.

In 1966 Angelou returned to California, where she wrote *Black, Blues, Black*, a 10-part television series about the role of African culture in American life. It aired in 1968. She also acted in several television productions, including the miniseries *Roots* (1977), and in such movies as *Poetic Justice* (1993) and *How to Make an American Quilt* (1995). In 1998 she made her directorial debut with *Down in the Delta* (1998).

Angelou's poetry, collected in such volumes as *Just Give Me a Cool Drink of Water 'fore I Diiie* (1971), *And Still I Rise* (1978), *Now Sheba Sings the Song* (1987), and *I Shall Not Be Moved* (1990), draws heavily on her personal history. She also wrote a book of meditations, *Wouldn't Take Nothing for My Journey Now* (1993), and an anecdote-filled book of advice to women entitled *Letter to My Daughter* (2008), even though her only biological child was male. Her children's books include *My Painted House, My Friendly Chicken and Me* (1994) and *Life Doesn't Frighten Me* (1998). The Maya's World series was published in 2004–05 and featured stories of children from various parts of the world.

In 1981 Angelou became a professor of American Studies at Wake Forest University in Winston-Salem, North Carolina. She was awarded the Presidential Medal of Freedom in 2011. She died on May 28, 2014, in Winston-Salem.

## ISAAC ASIMOV

(b. 1920—d. 1992)

The author of more than 400 books on a broad range of subjects, Isaac Asimov called himself a "born explainer." His streamlined versions of science facts are as popular as his science fiction, and his works include history and mysteries.

Isaac Asimov, 1991.

Asimov was born in Petrovichi, Russia, on January 2, 1920. His family moved to the United States when he was 3. When he was about 9, he began reading the science fiction magazines stocked in his parents' candy store in Brooklyn, New York. In 1938, while he was still a teenager, he sold his first short story, "Marooned Off

Vesta," to *Amazing Stories*.

After postgraduate work at Columbia University, Asimov began teaching biochemistry at Boston University in 1949. The next year his first books—the futuristic satire *Pebble in the Sky* and the thriller *I, Robot*—were published. As the pace and scope of his writing increased, he moved to New York City for a freelance career but retained his academic title.

Decades ahead of their time, Asimov's *The Intelligent Man's Guide to Science* (1960) and *Today and Tomorrow and...* (1973) are still popular with researchers. With his wife, Janet, he wrote a series of children's books about a mixed-up robot named Norby. Two volumes of autobiography—*In Memory Yet Green* and *In Joy Still Felt*—cover the years 1920 to 1954 and 1954 to 1978.

The more than 30 subjects in Asimov's How Did We Find Out series range from numbers (1973) to photosynthesis and microwaves (both 1989). Other subjects in the young people's series are dinosaurs, germs, volcanoes, DNA, and the brain. In 1989 he also published the novel *Nemesis*; *SciQuest selections, The Tyrannosaurus Prescription and 100 Other Essays*; and *Asimov on Science*, a collection of *Fantasy and Science Fiction* columns written over a 30-year period. He died in New York City on April 6, 1992.

## W.H. AUDEN

(b. 1907–d. 1973)

The eminent poet and man of letters W.H. Auden was regarded as a hero of the left in the 1930s. His poems, plays, and essays explored the realms of psychology, politics, and religion.

Wystan Hugh Auden was born in York, England, on February 21, 1907. He studied to be a mining engineer, but by 1922 he was determined to make poetry his career. From 1925 to 1928 he attended Oxford University, where he won recognition as an outstanding young poet. After studying in Germany for a year, he worked as a schoolmaster in England and Scotland for five years.

Auden established his reputation with the volume *Poems*, published in 1930. His psychological insight was matched by his attacks on capitalism and totalitarianism in *Look, Stranger!* (1936) and other works. He collaborated with Christopher Isherwood on plays including *The Ascent of F6* (1936). In the mid-1930s Auden married Erika Mann, daughter of the German novelist Thomas Mann, in order to secure a British passport for her, but they never lived together. Auden moved to New York City in 1939 and became a U.S. citizen in 1946. In these years his commitment to Christianity deepened. He wrote the Christmas oratorio *For the Time Being* (1944) and won a Pulitzer Prize for the poem *The Age of Anxiety* (1947). He spent much of his time in Italy and Austria and was a professor of poetry at Oxford from 1956 to 1961. In his later years Auden worked on opera libretti for several works, including Igor Stravinsky's *Rake's Progress* (1951), while he was active as a poet, teacher, lecturer, and essayist. He died in Vienna, Austria, on September 28, 1973.

# JANE AUSTEN

(b. 1775—d. 1817)

Through her portrayals of ordinary people in everyday life Jane Austen gave the genre of the novel its modern character. She began writing at an early age. At 15 she was writing plays and sketches for the amusement of her family, and by the time she was 21 she had begun to write novels that are among the finest in English literature.

Jane Austen was born on December 16, 1775, in the parsonage of Steventon, a village in Hampshire, England. She had six brothers and one sister. Her father, the Reverend George Austen, was a rector of the village. Although she and her sister briefly attended several different schools, Jane was educated mainly by her father, who taught his own children and several pupils who boarded with the family.

Her father retired when Jane was 25. By that time her brothers, two of whom later became admirals, had careers and families of their own. Jane, her sister, Cassandra, and their parents went to live in Bath. After the father's death in 1805, the family lived temporarily in Southampton

A portrait believed to be of English novelist Jane Austen, c. 1800.

before finally settling in Chawton.

All of Jane Austen's novels are love stories. However, neither Jane nor her sister ever married. There are hints of two or three romances in Jane's life, but little is known about them, for Cassandra destroyed all letters of a personal nature after Jane's death. The brothers had large families, and Jane was a favorite with her nephews and nieces.

Jane Austen wrote two novels before she was 22. These she later revised and published as *Sense and Sensibility* (1811) and *Pride and Prejudice* (1813). She completed her third novel, *Northanger Abbey*, when she was 27 or 28, but it did not appear in print until after her death. She wrote three more novels in her late 30s: *Mansfield Park* (1814), *Emma* (1816), and *Persuasion* (published together with *Northanger Abbey* in 1818).

She wrote of the world she knew. Her novels portray the lives of the gentry and clergy of rural England, and they take place in the country villages and neighborhoods, with an occasional visit to Bath and London. Her world was small, but she saw it clearly and portrayed it with wit and detachment. She described her writing as "the little bit (two inches wide) of ivory on which I work with so fine a brush, as produces little effect after much labor."

She died on July 18, 1817, after a long illness. She spent the last weeks of her life in Winchester, near her physician, and is buried in the cathedral there.

# JAMES BALDWIN

(b. 1924—d. 1987)

An American novelist, essayist, and playwright, James Baldwin wrote with eloquence and passion on the subject of race in America. His main message was that blacks deserve to be treated as equals and that the civil rights problem derives from the insecurity of the white man, who needs a "Negro" to whom he can feel superior.

James Arthur Baldwin was born on August 2, 1924, in the Harlem section of New York City, to David and Berdis Jones Baldwin. His father, a Sunday minister, was very strict with his nine children, of whom James was the oldest. Teachers remembered James as a slight, intelligent, sad-looking boy. After graduating from high school in 1942, he worked at various jobs. A literary fellowship in 1948 enabled him to go to Europe, where he lived mostly in France. *Go Tell It on the Mountain* (1953), an autobiographical novel, helped establish him as a writer.

After his return to the United States in 1957, Baldwin became deeply involved in the civil rights movement. *Nobody Knows My Name* (1961), a collection of essays, brought him awards. His play *Blues for Mister Charlie* was produced on Broadway in 1964. Baldwin also wrote the essay collections *Notes of a Native Son* (1955) and *The Fire Next Time* (1963); *Going to Meet the Man* (short stories, 1965); and the novels *Giovanni's Room* (1956), *Another Country* (1962), *Tell Me How Long the Train's Been Gone* (1968), *If Beale Street Could Talk* (1974), and *Just Above My Head* (1979). He died in St-Paul de Vence, France, on November 30, 1987.

# SAMUEL BECKETT

(b. 1906–d. 1989)

Unheroes grope their way through a surrealistic world in Samuel Beckett's plays and novels. Beckett, Irish by birth, wrote mostly in French, yet maintained an incomparable style when he translated his works into English.

Samuel Barclay Beckett was born on April 13, 1906. The younger of two sons, he grew up in Foxrock, a suburb of Dublin. His father, William Frank Beckett, was a surveyor who established his own firm in Dublin. His mother had been a nurse.

Young Samuel went to private Protestant schools. From about 1915 to 1919 he was a pupil at Earlsfort House School in Dublin. His skill at sports helped him make friends easily, and he was a brilliant pupil.

At Portora Royal School in Northern Ireland, Samuel was again outstanding. After getting his bachelor's degree at Trinity College in Dublin in 1927, he got a job teaching English at a school in Paris.

Beckett spent two years in Paris, where he fell in with the circle surrounding James Joyce. During this time Beckett's first published works appeared. One of them was *Whoroscope* (1930), a long poem. In 1930 he returned to Trinity College to teach French and do graduate work. At the end of 1931 he resigned his teaching job to travel and write.

Except for yearly visits to his family, Beckett never lived in Ireland again. For the next five years Beckett lived in France, England, and Germany. Beckett wrote a book of short stories (*More Pricks Than Kicks*, 1934) and a book of poems (*Echo's Bones*, 1935). In 1937 he settled permanently in Paris. His first novel, *Murphy*, came out in 1938.

In 1940 Beckett fled the German armies that occupied northern France. But he soon returned to Paris to join the Resistance. In 1942 his underground group was discovered by the Germans, but he escaped to unoccupied France.

In about 1945 Beckett turned to writing in French. His major works began to appear in the 1950s. A trilogy of novels (1951–53) was later translated into English as *Molloy*, *Malone Dies*, and *The Unnamable*. *Waiting for Godot*, first produced in 1953, brought Beckett world fame. It was a static approach to theater. Nothing much happened in the play, and nothing much was said. Yet it had a dramatic impact on audiences. Beckett used the same technique—called "theater of the absurd"—in *Endgame* (1957), *Krapp's Last Tape* (1958), *Happy Days* (1961), and *Play* (1963). He also wrote several more novels, including *How It Is* (1961). In 1969 he received the Nobel Prize in Literature. His last work was a limited-edition novella, *Stirrings Still* (1989). Beckett died in Paris on December 22, 1989.

# WILLIAM BLAKE

(b. 1757—d. 1827)

"I do not behold the outward creation.... it is a hindrance and not action." Thus William Blake—painter, engraver, and poet—explained why his work was filled with religious visions rather than with subjects from everyday life. Few people in his time realized that Blake expressed these visions with a talent that approached genius. He lived in near poverty and died unrecognized. Today, however, Blake is acclaimed as one of England's great figures of art and literature and one of the most inspired and original painters of his time.

Blake was born on November 28, 1757, in London. His father ran a hosiery shop. William, the third of five children, went to school only long enough to learn to read and write, and then he worked in the shop until he was 14. When he saw the boy's talent for drawing, Blake's father apprenticed him to an engraver.

At 25 Blake married Catherine Boucher. He taught her to read and write and to help him in his work. They had no children. They worked together to produce an edition of Blake's poems and drawings called *Songs of Innocence*. Blake engraved both words and pictures on copper printing plates. Catherine made the printing impressions, hand-colored the pictures, and bound the books. The books sold slowly, for a few shillings each. Today a single copy is worth many thousands of dollars.

Blake's fame as an artist and engraver rests largely on a set of 21 copperplate etchings to illustrate the Book of Job in the Old Testament. However, he did much work for which other artists and engravers got the credit. Blake was a poor businessman, and he preferred to work on subjects of his own choice rather than on those that publishers assigned him.

A follower of Emanuel Swedenborg, who offered a gentle and mystic interpretation of Christianity, Blake wrote poetry that largely reflects Swedenborgian views. *Songs of Innocence* (1789) shows life as it seems to innocent children. *Songs of Experience* (1794) tells of a mature person's realization of pain and terror in the universe. This book contains his famous

"Tiger! Tiger! Burning Bright." *Milton* (1804–08) and *Jerusalem* (1804–20) are longer and more obscure works. Blake died on August 12, 1827.

## JORGE LUIS BORGES

(b. 1899—d. 1986)

The Argentine writer Jorge Luis Borges is famous for his bizarre and fantastic stories. He was also a poet, an essayist-philosopher, a scholar-librarian, and a teacher.

Jorge Luis Borges was born in Buenos Aires on August 24, 1899, into a wealthy family. His father, Jorge Borges, was a lawyer and psychology professor, and his mother, who lived into her 90s, was a teacher and translator. For several years Jorge was educated at home by an English governess. He also spent many hours in the library of his English grandmother.

While the Borges family was visiting Switzerland in 1914, World War I broke out. Jorge went to school in Geneva, adding French and German to his Spanish and English. On graduating, he took a teacher-preparation course at Cambridge University in England.

From 1919 to 1921 the Borges family traveled in Spain. Borges wrote poetry and associated with a group of poets of the avant-garde Ultraist movement in Madrid. The return to Argentina was a moving experience for him. Some of this feeling was expressed in his first book of poems, *Fervor de Buenos Aires* (*The Passion of Buenos Aires*, 1923). When his father died in 1938, Borges took a job as a librarian. Soon afterward he began to write the short stories that were to make him famous. For opposing Juan Perón's dictatorship, Borges was fired from his library job. He found work teaching and continued to write. After the fall of Perón in 1955, Borges was named director of the National Library of Argentina. The next year he also was made a professor of literature at the University of Buenos Aires. He received Argentina's national prize for literature for 1956.

About this time Borges began to lose his sight because of a rare hereditary condition. Although he continued to write, usually by memorizing and then dictating his work, his output slowed. Nevertheless, his fame grew. Some of his books were translated and became popular in Europe. In 1967 Borges married Elsa Astete Millán, 40 years after their first meeting at the home of a mutual friend.

*Ficciones* (1962) and *Labyrinths* (1962) were the first Borges books to be translated into English. They contain some of his best stories. *Other Inquisitions* (1964) includes some of his best essays. Other Borges story collections include *The Aleph* (1970), *Doctor Brodie's Report* (1972), and *The Book of Sand* (1977). In 1980 Borges won the Cervantes Prize, which is Spain's highest literary award. He died on June 14, 1986, in Geneva, Switzerland.

## WILLIAM S. BURROUGHS

(b. 1914—d. 1997)

U.S. author and icon of popular culture William S. Burroughs was associated with the Beat Generation. His controversial and often satirical writings described a modern underworld of drugs and disillusionment.

William Seward Burroughs was born on February 5, 1914, in St. Louis, Missouri. His grandfather founded the Burroughs Adding Machine company, which later merged with Sperry Univac to form Unisys. He dreamed of becoming a writer as a young boy. His first literary endeavor was called *The Autobiography of a Wolf*, which he wrote after reading *The Biography of a Grizzly Bear*.

From there, Burroughs's interests and writing experiments ranged from gangster stories to tales of English high society. When he was 15 years old he was sent to the Los Alamos Ranch School, an activity-based camp and school, which he did not enjoy. Burroughs found Harvard University to be more to his liking, and while doing graduate work there in anthropology he wrote several unconventional short stories with his friends. He was married for the first time in 1937, to Ilse Herzfeld Klapper. They divorced in 1946.

In his early 30s Burroughs decided to join the gangster underground of

New York City, where he became addicted to heroin and was befriended by Herbert Huncke. In 1943 Burroughs met Jack Kerouac and Allen Ginsberg, who were then students at Columbia University. Huncke, Kerouac, and Ginsberg were leading figures of the Beat Generation—the name for a group of young literary nonconformists who experimented with alternative lifestyles and drugs in the 1950s. Although Burroughs was older than them, he was greatly influenced by their ideas, as they were by his. Burroughs and Kerouac collaborated on a novel that they chose not to publish.

From New York Burroughs moved to eastern Texas, where he lived with Huncke and Joan Vollmer Adams, who became his wife. Together with two children, one from Adams's first marriage and one the child of Adams and Burroughs, they lived on a farm where they fed their drug habits and grew oranges, cotton, and marijuana. Kerouac visited the farm and described his outlandish experiences there in *On the Road*. Burroughs himself did not produce any writing during this period.

From 1948 to 1951 Burroughs attended Mexico City College. During this time he wrote a hard-edged look at his life as a drug addict, *Junkie* (subtitled *Confessions of an Unredeemed Drug Addict*). Ginsberg arranged for the publication of *Junkie* as a pulp paperback in 1953 under Burroughs's pseudonym of William Lee; in 1964 it was reissued as *Junky* under Burroughs's name. He also wrote *Queer*, an autobiographical study of his homosexuality. *Queer* was not published until 1985.

Burroughs was fascinated with guns. He once shot a mouse in a bar with a pistol. At a drunken party in Mexico City in 1951, Burroughs proclaimed to his wife that it was time for their "William Tell" act. He pulled out a gun and attempted to shoot a cocktail glass off the top of Adams's head. He missed and shot her in the head from 6 feet (1.8 meters) away, killing her. The authorities punished him with a fine and a few weeks in jail.

This killing propelled Burroughs into a writing career; in his later years he said that he might never have become an author if he had not killed his wife. In 1959, two years after leaving a drug rehabilitation program, he published what many considered to be his masterpiece, *Naked Lunch*. The book was assembled in two weeks using what Burroughs called the "cut-up" technique. Similar to the montage method in painting, it consisted of him cutting random paragraphs and pages from his writings and gluing them together on a separate page. The result was a book without traditional form or structure, linked by images and recurring general themes.

*Naked Lunch* was nontraditional in content as well. Burroughs wrote about everything from bodily functions to political oppression to media manipulation. His topics were so controversial, in fact, that in 1965 the state of Massachusetts attempted to ban *Naked Lunch* on charges of obscenity. Authors Norman Mailer and Allen Ginsberg testified on behalf of the book, and the state lost its case. *Naked Lunch* was one of the last books of the period to lead to an obscenity trial.

Burroughs spent much of the 1960s traveling the world, living and writing in Morocco, South America, and other locations. Books published during that decade included *The Soft Machine* (1961), *The Ticket That Exploded* (1962), and *Nova Express* (1964). In much of his fiction, Burroughs used his addiction to drugs as a metaphor for other addictions he believed plagued society at that time, such as addictions to sex, money, and power.

Along with writing fiction, Burroughs recorded audio tapes of himself reading his work, often in combination with music. In *Call Me Burroughs* (1965), *You're the Man I Want to Share My Money With* (1981), and *The "Priest" They Called Him* (1992, with Kurt Cobain) and other recordings, Burroughs blurred the lines between poetry and narrative fiction. The rhythm and tone in which the words were spoken, as well as the words themselves, conveyed meaning.

Another novel, *The Wild Boys*, was published in 1971. Burroughs returned to the United States in 1974 and wrote his first straight narrative, *Cities of the Red Night* (1981). Along with it, two other books, *The Place of Dead Roads* (1984) and *The Western Lands* (1987), complete a thematic trilogy. In these books Burroughs examined humanity's ability to adapt to its future, which he believed inevitably included space and time travel. A volume of his correspondence, *Letters 1945–59*, was published in 1993, and a memoir called *My Education: A Book of Dreams* followed in 1994.

In 1991 David Cronenberg directed a film entitled *Naked Lunch*, which depicted Burroughs's real life and also incorporated aspects of the book. The film, extensive Internet exposure, and Burroughs's own life and work all contributed to his status as a cultural icon. Burroughs was appealing to many people looking for an alternative to the political and cultural status quo. He was an antihero and an underground curiosity, all the more interesting for his incongruous grandfatherly appearance and bizarre life experiences.

Burroughs struggled with drug addiction his entire adult life, repeatedly going through cures only to relapse months or years later. He died on August 2, 1997, in Lawrence, Kansas, at the age of 83.

# LORD BYRON

(b. 1788—d. 1824)

One of the most talked-of men of his day was George Gordon, Lord Byron. His handsome face, riotous living and many love affairs, and a tragic death at the age of 36 made him a romantic, fascinating figure to both men and women of the time. Today his reputation is chiefly as a poet.

George Gordon was born on January 22, 1788, in London. His great-uncle, from whom he inherited his title, was known as "wicked" Lord Byron; and his father, an army officer, was called "mad Jack." Born with an abnormally formed foot, he was sensitive about his appearance all his life. When he was three years old his father died, leaving the boy and his mother nearly penniless.

Byron succeeded to the title of baron when he was 10. The honor brought with it a half-ruined estate, Newstead Abbey, and a moderate income. At 17 he entered Cambridge University. He read much literature but cared little for other subjects. Determined to overcome his physical disability, Byron became a good rider, swimmer, boxer, and marksman.

His first collection of poetry, published when he was 19, was a volume called *Hours of Idleness*. It was attacked by the *Edinburgh Review*. Byron responded with a satire entitled *English Bards and Scotch Reviewers.* His travels in Europe and the Middle East inspired his first long poem, *Childe Harold's Pilgrimage*. The first two sections were published in 1812, and he became famous almost overnight. Women sought him out, and young men copied his style of wearing an open collar and flowing cravat.

In 1815 he married Anne Milbanke. They had one daughter but soon separated. The public reacted unfavorably to Byron's often scandalous conduct, and in a fit of temper he left England for Italy. There he wrote additional cantos for *Childe Harold*; *Manfred*, a verse play; and *Don Juan*, a half-romantic, half-humorous poetic version of the old Spanish story. Byron became interested in Greece's struggle to free itself from Turkish rule, and he went to Greece to help organize the revolt. He died of a fever at Missolonghi (now Mesolongion) on April 19, 1824.

# TRUMAN CAPOTE

(b. 1924—d.1984)

American novelist, short-story writer, and playwright Truman Capote was noted for creating eccentric characters and highlighting bizarre situations in his work. His popular books include the charmingly offbeat *Breakfast at Tiffany's* and the journalistic novel *In Cold Blood*.

Truman Streckfus Persons was born on September 30, 1924, in New Orleans, Louisiana. His father, Julian, was a former riverboat employee turned businessman. When Truman was about four, his parents were divorced. He grew up among relatives in different parts of the South. Later his mother married Joseph Garcia Capote, a businessman in the East. At about age 11, Truman began attending school in New York City and later in Greenwich, Connecticut.

Truman was not very interested in school, but he did like to write. After graduating at age 17, he went to New Orleans, then to New York City to write and work. In 1945 his stories began to appear in magazines. They won him two O. Henry awards. His first books were *Other Voices, Other Rooms* (published in 1948), a novel about an adolescent boy in a run-down Southern mansion, and *A Tree of Night* (1949), a collection of short stories.

Capote's fantasy *The Grass Harp* (1951) featured a fight over a home dropsy-cure business. He rewrote it as a play in 1952. He also wrote the book and lyrics for composer Harold Arlen's musical comedy, *House of Flowers* (1954). In his short novel *Breakfast at Tiffany's* (1958), Capote created one of his most unforgettable characters—Manhattan playgirl Holly Golightly. The movie version came out in 1961. In 1966 a television presentation of his short story "A Christmas Memory" won a Peabody award.

Capote became interested in journalism and focused his attention on the brutal murder of a Kansas farm family. For several years he investigated the case, talking to everyone connected with the killing. The result was *In Cold Blood* (1966), which he called a "nonfiction novel." Although it was based on fact, it read like suspense fiction and became immensely popular. It was produced as a movie in 1967. *Then It All Came Down* (1976) also deals with crime and criminal justice.

*Music for Chameleons* (1980) is a mixed collection of short stories, essays, and journalistic reporting. At the time of his death in Los Angeles, California, on August 25, 1984, he left unfinished *Answered Prayers*, a fictionalized account of his jet-set friends. The book was published as *Answered Prayers: The Unfinished Novel* in 1986, and it has since been reissued many times.

## LEWIS CARROLL

(b. 1832—d. 1898)

British author, mathematician, and logician Charles Dodgson, best known by his pen name of Lewis Carroll, is renowned for writing two of the most famous and admired children's books in the world: *Alice's Adventures in Wonderland* (1865) and its sequel, *Through the Looking-Glass* (1871). He also wrote poetry for children, including the famous nonsense poem *The Hunting of the Snark* (1876).

Charles Lutwidge Dodgson was born on January 27, 1832, in Daresbury, Cheshire, England. Charles was the eldest son of 11 children—four boys and seven girls. When he was 12 years old, he attended Richmond School, and two years later he entered Rugby School. Dodgson, being shy and having a stutter, found these four years of public school rough.

When Dodgson was 18, he entered Christ Church, Oxford University, where he studied, worked, and lived for the rest of his life. There he excelled in his studies, taking bachelor's and master's degrees, was ordained a deacon of the Church of England, and taught mathematics to several generations of Oxford students. Dodgson never married, and his few adult friends were mainly fellow faculty members. His hobbies were mathematical puzzles and photography.

Dodgson always loved children. In his youth, he had spent much of his time inventing games to play with his younger brothers and sisters. As an adult, he often gave parties for children and took them to the theater and on picnics. On one such picnic in 1862 his guests were Alice, Lorina, and Edith, the daughters of Henry George Liddell, dean of Christ Church College. On this hot summer day, in a meadow along the River Isis, Dodgson began to tell them the "Alice" stories. Later he wrote them out for the children, and the manuscript tales were read and reread by many people. *Alice's Adventures in Wonderland* was published in 1865, and *Through the Looking-Glass* appeared in 1871 (although it was dated 1872). Both were illustrated by the famous cartoonist and artist John Tenniel. Both were also published under Dodgson's pen name, which he created by translating his first and middle names, Charles and Lutwidge, into Latin as Carolus Ludovicus, and then reversing and retranslating them into English.

In 1876 Dodgson published *The Hunting of the Snark*, the amusing subtitle of which is *An Agony in Eight Fits*. Other children's books that he wrote were *Sylvie and Bruno* (1889) and *Sylvie and Bruno Concluded* (1893). To these books he signed his pen name; for several other works on mathematics and logic he used his real name. His book royalties enabled him to teach fewer classes, and he spent his summers at Eastbourne on the seacoast. Dodgson died on January 14, 1898, in Guildford, Surrey, England.

# RAYMOND CARVER

(b. 1938—d. 1988)

Raymond Carver was an American short-story writer and poet whose realistic writings about the working poor mirrored his own life.

Carver was the son of a sawmill worker. He married a year after finishing high school and supported his wife and two children by working as a janitor, gas-station attendant, and delivery man. He became seriously interested in a writing career after taking a creative-writing course at Chico State College (now California State University, Chico) in 1958. His short stories began to appear in magazines while he studied at Humboldt State College (now Humboldt State University) in Arcata, California (B.A., 1963). Carver's first success as a writer came in 1967 with the story "Will You Please Be Quiet, Please?," and he began writing full-time after losing his job as a textbook editor in 1970. The highly successful short-story collection *Will You Please Be Quiet, Please?* (1976) established his reputation.

Carver began drinking heavily in 1967 and was repeatedly hospitalized for alcoholism in the 1970s, while continuing to turn out short stories. After conquering his drinking problem in the late 1970s, he taught for several years at the University of Texas at El Paso and at Syracuse University, and in 1983 he won a literary award whose generous annual stipend freed him to again concentrate on his writing full-time. His later short-story collections were *What We Talk About When We Talk About Love* (1981), *Cathedral* (1984), and *Where I'm Calling From* (1988). While his short stories were what made his critical reputation, he was also an accomplished poet in the realist tradition of Robert Frost. Carver's poetry collections include *At Night the Salmon Move* (1976), *Where Water Comes Together with Other Water* (1985), and *Ultramarine* (1986). He died of lung cancer at age 50.

In his short stories Carver chronicled the everyday lives and problems of the working poor in the Pacific Northwest. His blue-collar characters are crushed by broken marriages, financial problems, and failed careers, but they are often unable to understand or even articulate their own anguish. Carver's stripped-down, minimalist prose style is remarkable for its honesty and power. He is credited with helping revitalize the genre of the English-language short story in the late 20th century.

However, controversy arose over the nature of Carver's writing—and even his lasting literary reputation—in the early 21st century. It was revealed that his long-time editor, Gordon Lish, had drastically changed many of Carver's early stories. While Lish's significant involvement in Carver's writing had long been suspected, the extent of his editing became public knowledge when, in 2007, Carver's widow, the poet Tess Gallagher, announced that she was seeking to publish the original versions of the stories in *What We Talk About When We Talk About Love* (which appeared as *Beginners* in the U.K. and also as part of the Library of America's *Raymond Carver: Collected Stories* [both 2009]). Lish was shown to have changed characters' names, cut the length of many stories (over 75 percent of the text in two cases), and altered the endings of some stories. However, most of Carver's famously terse sentences were his own, as was the hallmark bleak working-class milieu of the short stories.

# MIGUEL DE CERVANTES

(b. 1547—d. 1616)

Some 400 years ago Miguel de Cervantes wrote a book that made him the most important figure in Spanish literature to this day. Six editions of *Don Quixote* were printed in the first year after the publication of the first part (1605). Translations into foreign languages were begun almost immediately. It is one of the most popular books ever written.

The career of Miguel de Cervantes stands in striking contrast to the fate of his great book. It was one long struggle against poverty, debt, and sheer bad luck. Little is known of his first 20 years. He was born in the town of Alcalá de Henares, near Madrid, in the autumn of 1547. His father, Rodrigo de Cervantes, was a poor and obscure surgeon. There is no evidence that Miguel attended the university of his native town or of any other of the towns in which he spent his youth—Valladolid, Seville, and Madrid.

By the end of 1569, when he was 22, Cervantes was in Rome. There for a time he served as a gentleman-in-waiting in the household of Cardinal Acquaviva. The next year he enlisted in the Spanish militia, then on duty in Italy. In October 1571 he took part in the battle of Lepanto, a famous sea fight in which the allied fleets of Spain and the Italian cities destroyed the Turkish fleet. In this battle Cervantes suffered three gunshot wounds, one of which permanently crippled his left hand.

Four years later the ship on which Cervantes was returning to Spain was captured by Barbary pirates. He and his brother were carried as slaves to Algiers. Although his brother was able to earn his freedom relatively quickly, Miguel was held for several more years. He made several unsuccessful attempts to escape and partly as a result of those attempts became known for his bravery and leadership among the community of captives.

After five years of slavery, Cervantes was at last ransomed by his relatives and friends and returned to Spain. With a maimed hand, he could not continue soldiering, and the king turned a deaf ear to his requests for an appointment; so he tried writing. In the next few years he turned out 20 or 30 plays as well as a pastoral romance, *Galatea*. But they were all failures, more or less. This convinced Cervantes that he could never earn his bread by his pen. Meanwhile his father had died, and Cervantes had married a girl who brought him a small dowry.

By 1587 Cervantes was again in the king's service—this time as an agent to collect wheat, barley, and oil for the fleet of ships known as the Spanish Armada, which was defeated the next year by the "sea hawks" of England. In this and like capacities he served the king for several years, though his pay was long overdue. He often experienced financial difficulties.

For a few months in 1597–98 Cervantes was imprisoned because he could not make up for a shortage in his accounts as tax collector, caused by the failure of the banker to whom he had entrusted the money. He may have conceived of the idea for *Don Quixote* while he was in prison. Apparently he was jailed again in about 1603, but nothing certain is known about these years. In 1604 he came to Valladolid with the manuscript of the first part of *Don Quixote*.

*Don Quixote de la Mancha* is the story of an elderly gentleman of La

Mancha, the bare and monotonous plateau of central Spain. He reads so many of the exaggerated romances of chivalry of his day that he finally believes them to be true. One day he sets forth himself as a knight-errant on his old horse, Rosinante. A shrewd, good-natured peasant of his village, Sancho Panza, goes with him as his squire. Don Quixote's overly romantic view of the world contrasts with the realistic and practical view of Sancho Panza as they experience a series of comic adventures. The influence of the book was so great, even in translation, that the word "quixotic," meaning "foolishly impractical" or "idealistic," became part of the English language.

The first part of the book was published in 1605, when Cervantes was 57. Despite its huge success, he received little money because he sold his rights in the book to his publisher. While the fame of *Don Quixote* spread through Europe, Cervantes lived in poverty, dependent upon rich patrons. He published the second part of *Don Quixote* in 1615 and died the following year.

In addition to *Don Quixote* Cervantes published several other popular works. These included a collection of short fiction entitled *Novelas ejemplares* (1613; *Exemplary Novels*) and his last romance, *Los trabaios de Persiles y Sigismunda, historia setentrional* (*The Labors of Persiles and Sigismunda: A Northern Story*), which was published posthumously in 1617. It is through *Don Quixote*, however, that Cervantes made his greatest and most lasting contribution to literature.

# RAYMOND CHANDLER

(b. 1888—d. 1959)

American author Raymond Chandler wrote detective stories. He was best known as the creator of the private detective Philip Marlowe, whom he characterized as a poor but honest upholder of ideals in an opportunistic and sometimes brutal society in Los Angeles, California.

Raymond Thornton Chandler was born on July 23, 1888, in Chicago, Illinois. From 1896 to 1912 he lived in England with his mother, a British subject of Irish birth. Although Chandler was an American citizen and a resident of California when World War I began in 1914, he served in the Canadian army and then in the Royal Flying Corps (later the Royal Air Force). After returning to California in 1919, he prospered as a petroleum company executive until the Great Depression of the 1930s, when he turned to writing for a living. His first published short story appeared in the pulp magazine *Black Mask* in 1933. From 1943 Chandler was a Hollywood screenwriter. Among his best-known scripts were for the films *Double Indemnity* (1944), *The Blue Dahlia* (1946), and *Strangers on a Train* (1951)—the last written in collaboration with Czenzi Ormonde.

Chandler completed seven novels, all with Philip Marlowe as the main character: *The Big Sleep* (1939), *Farewell, My Lovely* (1940), *The High Window* (1942), *The Lady in the Lake* (1943), *The Little Sister* (1949), *The Long Goodbye* (1953), and *Playback* (1958). Among his numerous short-story collections are *Five Murderers* (1944) and *The Midnight Raymond Chandler* (1971). The most popular film versions of Chandler's work were *Murder, My Sweet* (1944; also distributed as *Farewell, My Lovely*), starring Dick Powell, and *The Big Sleep* (1946), starring Humphrey Bogart and Lauren Bacall, both film noir classics. Chandler died on March 26, 1959, in La Jolla, California.

## GEOFFREY CHAUCER

(b. 1343—d. 1400)

For six centuries Geoffrey Chaucer has retained his status in the highest rank of the English poets. As many-sided as William Shakespeare, he did for English narrative what Shakespeare did for drama. If he lacks the profundity of Shakespeare, he excels in playfulness of mood and simplicity of expression. His foremost characteristics are his skillful creation of realistic characters and his humor: by turns twinkling, quietly glowing, or loudly robust. Although his language, Middle English, is difficult to read and his usage often seems quaint he was an essentially modern writer, and his works still speak to modern readers.

As a soldier, diplomat, justice of the peace, member of Parliament, and man of affairs Chaucer lived a full and busy life. It is as a writer, however, that he is remembered today. Many of the people he met in the course of his career influenced his writing, and his familiarity with and mastery of all genres of medieval literature gave him the means to communicate his view of the world with humor and intelligence.

Geoffrey Chaucer was born in London, probably in 1342 or 1343. He was the son of Agnes de Copton and John Chaucer, a prosperous wine merchant. In 1357, while he was in his teens, Geoffrey was a page in the household of Prince Lionel, son of King Edward III. This is known from an entry in the household account book of Countess Elizabeth, Lionel's wife, that records the purchase of a suit of clothes for Geoffrey Chaucer. Two years later Chaucer was with an army that King Edward led into France during the Hundred Years' War. He was taken prisoner by the French but was soon ransomed by the king for a large sum.

Of his next seven years, nothing definite is known, but there is reason to believe that he may have been studying law in London. By 1367 he was married and a member of the royal household with the rank of yeoman. Later he became a squire, with a regular pension, or salary. His wife, Philippa, was a member of the queen's household. Thus as a young man Chaucer had already embarked on the career as an official that he was to follow for the remainder of his life. He wrote his first significant poem, *The Book of the Duchess*, in 1369 or 1370, on the occasion of the death from plague of the first wife of John of Gaunt, another of Edward's sons. The poem was written as a dream allegory, or dream vision, in which an allegorical tale is presented in the narrative framework of a dream.

Between 1370 and 1378 Chaucer was sent on seven missions to France, Flanders, and Italy. In Italy he came into contact with the works of three writers who were to influence him profoundly: Dante, Petrarch, and Boccaccio. In his best poem of the decade, *House of Fame* (1374–79; unfinished), he established the light, bantering tone that is his signature style. In 1374 he assumed the office of comptroller of the customs and subsidy of wools, skins, and tanned hides for the Port of London. In 1382 he became comptroller for wine and other merchandise. During this time he wrote a work on love, *Parliament of Fowls* (1380). In 1385 he was appointed justice of the peace, and in 1386 he sat for one term in Parliament. His other works of this period are *Troilus and Criseyde* (1382–86), from a story by Boccaccio, and *Legend of Good Women* (1385–87).

Chaucer's life was difficult during the period from 1386 to 1389, when the political situation in England was unsettled. Adding to his difficulty was the death of his wife in 1387. When Richard II gained control of the country in 1389, Chaucer's fortunes changed for the better. During this period he began his masterpiece, *The Canterbury Tales*.

From 1389 to 1391 he had a succession of responsible posts. As clerk of the king's works, he was put in charge of Westminster Palace, the Tower of London, and other palaces and manors. He was given a commission to survey the roads, bridges, and ditches along the Thames near London, and he was put in charge of repairs to St. George's Chapel at Windsor. A less exacting post fell to him in 1391, when he was made subforester of one of the king's parks. He held this position until his death on October 25, 1400. Not long before his death he purchased a house in the garden of Westminster Abbey. He was buried in the abbey—a great honor for a commoner—in a section that came to be known in later centuries as the Poets' Corner.

Born soon after the beginning of the Hundred Years' War, Chaucer lived through the terrible years of the plague known as the Black Death, through troubled times for the government, and through challenges to the established church. Chaucer's career allowed him to have access to people and ideas beyond the ordinary scope of a common Englishman of the time. Literature of all eras delighted him. Ovid, Virgil, Livy, Boethius, Petrarch, Dante, and Jean de Meun are among the authors who most influenced him. Taking what he needed from others, he remolded and immortalized it, with great narrative skill.

Chaucer met people from all stations in society and all walks of life. In his England of expanding trade with all nations he met shipman, merchant, overseer, and plowman. In an era of changing religious ideas, he met men and women of various clerical orders, from priest and nun to abbot and abbess. He may have known John Wycliffe, who was a forerunner of the Protestant Reformation. As a page and later as a courtier, Chaucer became acquainted with the nobility and with royalty. His wife was a lady in waiting. As a soldier he knew hardship and foreign captivity. He was familiar with the lore and customs of chivalry, without taking them entirely seriously.

Chaucer knew men of law and doctors of medicine, and may even have studied these professions as a young man He knew innkeepers, and on their premises may well have lifted a cup of the very wine that his father had sold to them. On trips to the continent he mingled with men of high estate who were directing the affairs of nations. All of these gave him inspiration for the characters he created in his writing.

Several languages and dialects were in use in Chaucer's England. Latin was the language of the church. Most learned books were written in Latin and copied out by scribes, as the printing press did not yet exist. An Anglo-Norman dialect of the French language was used in the royal court and the courts of law. An early form of English—now called Middle English—was the language of the common people. Chaucer chose to write in English and was the first court writer to do so. As a Londoner he used the English of the Midland counties. This was one of several regional dialects that coexisted then because there was so little contact between the various parts of the country. Modern English has more in common with Chaucer's dialect than with the other dialects of Middle English, perhaps due in part to the influence of his literary works.

Chaucer invented a new method of versifying: the rime royal, which is a seven-line stanza rhyming ababbcc. He also borrowed heavily from Latin and French when English words would not suffice. Many of these words do not look foreign to modern readers because they have long since become part of the ordinary English vocabulary—thanks in large part to Chaucer's influence.

# JOHN CHEEVER

(b. 1912—d. 1982)

American short-story writer and novelist John Cheever used his work to explore the material satisfactions and spiritual frustrations of modern upper-middle-class life. He has been called "the Chekhov of the suburbs"—referring to Russian playwright and master short-story writer Anton Chekhov—for his ability to capture the drama and sadness of the lives of his characters by revealing the undercurrents of apparently insignificant events. Known as a moralist, Cheever judges his characters from

John Cheever.

the standpoint of traditional morality.

Cheever was born on May 27, 1912, in Quincy, Massachusetts, into a middle-class family. His father worked in the shoe business, which was then booming in New England. With the eventual failure of that industry and the difficulties of his parents' marriage, Cheever had an unhappy adolescence. When he was 17 years old he was expelled from the Thayer Academy in Massachusetts; that event provided the theme for his first published story, "Expelled," which appeared in the *New Republic* in 1930.

During the Great Depression Cheever lived in Greenwich Village in New York, New York. He married in 1941 and had three children. In 1942, during World War II, Cheever enlisted in the army to train as an infantryman, but the army soon reassigned him to the Signal Corps as a scriptwriter for training films. After the war Cheever and his wife moved from New York City to the suburbs, whose culture and moral attitudes are often examined in his subsequent fiction.

Cheever's name was closely associated with the *New Yorker*, a periodical that published many of his stories, but his works also appeared in the *New Republic*, *Collier's*, *Story*, and the *Atlantic* magazines. A master of the short story, Cheever was famous for his clear and elegant prose and his careful fashioning of incidents and anecdotes. He is perhaps best-known for the two stories "The Enormous Radio" (1947) and "The Swimmer" (1964; filmed 1968). In the former story a young couple discovers that their new radio receives the conversations of other people in their apartment building. In "The Swimmer" a suburban man decides to swim his way home in the backyard pools of his neighbors and finds on the way that he is a lost soul. Cheever's first collection of short stories, *The Way Some People Live* (1943), was followed by many other collections, including *The Enormous Radio and Other Stories* (1953) and *The Brigadier and the Golf Widow* (1964). *The Stories of John Cheever* (1978) won the Pulitzer Prize for Fiction.

Cheever also wrote several novels. His first, *The Wapshot Chronicle* (1957), was a satire on several subjects, including the misuses of wealth and psychology. It earned him the National Book Award. Its sequel, *The Wapshot Scandal* (1964), was less successful. *Falconer* (1977) is the dark tale of a drug-addicted college professor who is imprisoned for murdering his brother. *Oh What a Paradise It Seems* (1982) is an elegiac story about a New Englander's efforts to preserve the quality of his life and that of a mill town's pond. Cheever died on June 18, 1982, in Ossining, New York. The book *The Letters of John Cheever*, edited by his son Benjamin Cheever, was published in 1988, and in 1991 *The Journals of John Cheever* appeared.

# ANTON CHEKHOV

(b. 1860—d. 1904)

The stories and plays written by Anton Chekhov describe in almost sociological detail the Russian society of his day. However, modern readers value his works chiefly for their deep insight into human emotion. Such is his subtlety that it is often difficult to decide whether a particular work is a comedy or a tragedy.

Anton Pavlovich Chekhov was born on January 29 (Janurary 17 according to the calendar in use at the time), 1860, at Taganrog, Russia, a port on the Sea of Azov. In 1879, after completing secondary school, he moved to Moscow. There he qualified as a physician and began to write humorous short pieces for journals. The first fruit of his literary maturity was an autobiographical story called "Step" ("The Steppe"), published in 1888. In 1890 he set off for remote Sakhalin Island, a penal colony off the

Pacific coast of Siberia, where he researched and wrote a classic study of the penal system.

In 1892 he moved to the village of Melikhovo, 50 miles (80 kilometers) south of Moscow, where he lived until 1898. During this period many of his finest short stories were published, including "Palata No. 6" ("Ward Number Six") and "Sosedi" ("Neighbors") (both 1892), "Chorny monakh" ("The Black Monk," 1894), "Ubiystvo" ("Murder") and "Ariadna" ("Ariadne") (both 1895), "Moya zhizn" ("My Life," 1896), and "Chelovek v futlyare" ("The Man in a Case," 1898).

Following an attack of tuberculosis, Chekhov retired in about 1898 to the resort city of Yalta on the Crimean coast. In search of an even milder climate he made frequent visits to the French Riviera. Despite these efforts, the disease took his life at Badenweiler, Germany, on July 15 (July 2), 1904.

During the last seven years of his life Chekhov gave four dramatic masterpieces to the world. *Dyadya Vanya* (*Uncle Vanya*) (finished about 1896) is a reworking of an earlier Chekhov play. *Chayka* (*The Seagull*) was first performed in 1896. *Tri sestry* (*Three Sisters*) dates from 1901 and *Vishnyovy sad* (*The Cherry Orchard*) from 1904. Chekhov also wrote thousands of letters that are now esteemed as literature.

## JOSEPH CONRAD

(b. 1857—d. 1924)

At the age of 20, Polish-born Joseph Conrad could speak no English; yet in his lifetime he would write outstanding novels and stories in that language. His tales of seafaring life depicted the concerns of all people: hazards in nature, the need for loyalty, and the danger in greed.

He was born Jósef Teodor Konrad Korzeniowski to a Polish family on December 3, 1857, in what is now Ukraine. He was orphaned in 1869 and was brought up by his uncle, who hoped that he would become a lawyer. But Conrad wanted to be a sailor. In October 1874 he moved to Marseille, France, and went to sea at age 17. In July 1876 he sailed as steward on the St-Antoine. It is likely that he took part in the smuggling of weapons, as later described in his novel *Nostromo*. It is known that in 1878 he was recovering from a mysterious chest wound that his uncle claimed was self-inflicted. Conrad, however, encouraged people to think he had suffered the injury in a duel.

In April 1878 he was sufficiently recovered to be a deckhand on the British freighter Mavis, and for the next 16 years he served in the British merchant navy. In 1886 he became eligible to be a ship's captain and also received British citizenship. His sea travels often took him to East Asia, and his experiences provided him with material for the novels and stories he would later write.

Back in London in 1889, he began his first novel, *Almayer's Folly*, but interrupted this work to visit Africa—a dream he had had since childhood. He commanded a steamboat on the Congo River, and, though he became very ill for awhile, the adventure provided him with the seed of his most famous story, the novella *Heart of Darkness*, published in 1899.

Under his anglicized name of Joseph Conrad, he published *Almayer's Folly* in April 1895. It did not sell well but got critical praise. However, he was soon to write his finest novels—*Lord Jim* (1900), *Nostromo* (1904), *Secret Agent* (1907), and *Under Western Eyes* (1911). In 1919 he settled in Bishopsbourne, England, where he died on August 3, 1924. His influence was felt long after his death.

## STEPHEN CRANE

(b. 1871—d. 1900)

A novelist, poet, and short-story writer, Stephen Crane is considered one of the most outstanding American novelists and short-story writers of the 19th century. He is regarded as a pioneer of social and psychological realism in American literature.

Crane was born in Newark, New Jersey, on November 1, 1871, into a family in which there were many Methodist ministers. He rebelled against the family's morality, but his writings were to reflect his religious background. His schooling was sporadic; nonetheless he read all of the 19th-century English writers and the Greek and Latin classics.

Crane worked as a freelance writer in New York City in the early 1890s, and there he wrote *Maggie: a Girl of the Streets*, first published in 1893. The novel, about an abused slum girl's descent into prostitution and her eventual suicide, displayed a realism that set the literary trend of the following generation. He then wrote *The Red Badge of Courage* (1895), which he intended to be "a psychological portrayal of fear." Crane also achieved mastery of the short story. His volumes of them include *The Little Regiment*, and *Other Episodes of the American Civil War* (1896) and *The Open Boat, and Other Tales of Adventure* (1898).

Crane's poetry was of a rhymeless, rhythmic, free-form style. He also did journalistic reporting in Greece and Cuba. Crane died on June 5, 1900, in Badenweiler, Germany, of tuberculosis, compounded by a recurring malarial fever he had contracted in Cuba while reporting on the Spanish-American War.

# DANIEL DEFOE

(b. 1660—d. 1731)

English novelist, pamphleteer, and journalist Daniel Defoe was perhaps best known as the author of *Robinson Crusoe*. This mythic tale of a man stranded on a desert island became an immediate success and an enduring classic, and Defoe became known as the father of the English novel. A man of many talents, he was not only a writer but also a businessman and a secret agent.

Defoe was born in London, England, in 1660. His father, James Foe, was a fairly prosperous chandler. The Foes were Dissenters, or Nonconformists, who did not believe in certain practices of the Church of England. At age 14 Daniel was sent to a Dissenters' academy. In addition to the traditional Latin and Greek, he studied French, Italian, Spanish, and history and became especially well educated in geography. He studied for the ministry but instead went into business. Engaged in financial speculation and foreign trade, he visited France and lived in Spain for a time. By his mid-30s, he began to use the name Defoe, which may have been a variant of the family's original Flemish name.

Meanwhile, Defoe began writing about public affairs. In witty and often bold pamphlets, verse, and periodicals, he called for reforms and advances in religious practices, economics, social welfare, and politics. In his *Essay on Projects*, written in 1698, he suggested a national bank, reformed bankruptcy laws, asylums, and academies of learning. He stressed the need for tolerance, often using satire for emphasis. In the enormously witty poem *The True-Born Englishman* of 1701, he assailed his country's prejudice against its foreign-born king, William III.

In 1702 Defoe wrote a pamphlet titled *The Shortest-Way with the Dissenters*, satirizing the Tories' persecution of Dissenters. Infuriated, the government had him fined, locked in a pillory, and imprisoned in 1703. After some months in prison he was released through the influence of Robert Harley, a statesman who became his patron. Defoe then wrote political pamphlets for Harley and served as his secret agent in working for the union of Scotland and England.

In 1704 Defoe started and almost single-handedly wrote the *Review*. It was the first of many "essay periodicals"—forerunners of the modern newspaper—with which he was connected. In the *Review*, Defoe discussed politics, general current affairs, religion, trade, manners, morals, and other matters. He published it until 1713.

Late in life Defoe began yet another career, writing fiction. As a novelist, he was celebrated for his insight into human nature. His plain, direct style and an accumulation of concrete, realistic details make his stories seem true to life. His lifelong love of travel and adventure is reflected in his "true histories" of pirates and thieves, in which he spiced facts with imagination. In 1719 he published the novel *Robinson Crusoe*, which was drawn partly from the memoirs of castaways, especially the Scottish sailor Alexander Selkirk. His other major works include two published in 1722: *Moll Flanders*, a novel that vividly recounts the urban struggles of its streetwise title character, and *A Journal of the Plague Year*, a fictionalized account of London's Great Plague of 1664–65. Defoe published his final novel, *Roxana*, in 1724. He died in London on April 24, 1731.

# DON DELILLO

(b. 1936—d. )

Prolific postmodern novelist Don DeLillo used rhythmic, artfully constructed sentences to depict 20th-century American culture with humor and acuity. His works were popular and highly regarded by critics.

Don DeLillo was born on November 20, 1936, to Italian immigrant parents and was raised in the Italian-American neighborhood of Fordham in the Bronx, New York. The family shared a narrow, three-story house with an aunt and uncle and their three children.

DeLillo found Cardinal Hayes High School boring and did not become seriously interested in literature until the summer of his 18th year. He worked as a playground attendant that summer and he brought books by Ernest Hemingway, William Faulkner, and James Joyce to read on the job. DeLillo then attended Fordham College, where he majored in communication arts. Although he was not particularly stimulated by his academic pursuits, in college DeLillo became more conscious of the cultural life of New York City, with its live jazz, abstract expressionist paintings, foreign films, anarchist poets, and rich variety of people.

After graduating from Fordham in 1959, DeLillo moved to the Murray Hill section of New York City and took a job writing copy for Ogilvy, Benson & Mather, an advertising agency, where he stayed until 1964. He had written a few short stories by that time. After leaving Ogilvy, DeLillo took freelance jobs to earn a living and began work on his first novel, *Americana*, which was published in 1971. *Americana* is the story of David Bell, a young executive who becomes disillusioned with corporate life and goes on a road trip to discover himself and the nation. Many trademark elements of DeLillo's fiction were apparent in his first novel, including satire and a portrait of an individual struggling against the masses.

DeLillo followed up *Americana* with two more books in the next two years: *End Zone* (1972) and *Great Jones Street* (1973). In 1975 he married Barbara Bennett, and the couple moved to Toronto, Ontario. The next year he published *Ratner's Star*, which was followed by *Players* in 1977 and *Running Dog* in 1978.

DeLillo's next novel was *The Names* (1982). *The Names* was written during a three-year period in which DeLillo lived in Greece and traveled throughout the Middle East and India. Upon his return to the United States in 1982 he began working on *White Noise*, which was published in 1985. His next and perhaps most controversial novel was *Libra* (1988), a fictionalized account of the assassination of President John F. Kennedy. DeLillo spent a year researching the assassination and Lee Harvey Oswald, who was accused of the crime. *Libra* questions whether Oswald acted alone or in conspiracy with the Central Intelligence Agency.

Because DeLillo did not normally encourage extensive media coverage of himself—he did not do a promotional tour until *Libra* was published—he was often labeled a recluse, as were the writers J.D. Salinger and Thomas Pynchon. In reality, DeLillo was much more accessible than either of those authors, and he consented to many interviews over the years. He did not seek out media attention, but neither did he usually reject it.

In addition to his novels, DeLillo wrote many short stories and a play, *The Day Room* (1987). In 1992 he published his first novella, *Pafko at the Wall*, in *Harper's Magazine*. Another novel, *Mao II*, was published in 1991, followed by a six-year hiatus from publishing during which DeLillo wrote *Underworld* (1997).

*Underworld* used *Pafko at the Wall* as the introduction and springboard for the story of Nick Shay, a waste-management specialist in corporate America who as a teenager had shot a waiter in the Bronx. *Underworld* was highly acclaimed as a sweeping portrait of the American psyche during the Cold War period. DeLillo was honored with many awards during his career, including the 1985 National Book Award for fiction for *White Noise* and the 1992 PEN/Faulkner award for *Mao II*.

# PHILIP K. DICK

(b. 1928—d. 1982)

American science-fiction author Philip K. Dick wrote novels and short stories that often depicted the psychological struggles of characters trapped in environments that are actually illusions. He was highly productive, often completing a new work—usually a short story or a novella—every two weeks for printing in pulp paperback collections. Many of his works were turned into popular movies.

Philip Kindred Dick was born on December 16, 1928, in Chicago, Illinois. He worked briefly in radio before studying at the University of California at Berkeley for one year. The publication of his first story, "Beyond Lies the Wub," in 1952 launched his full-time writing career. He published his first novel, *Solar Lottery*, in 1955. In such novels as *Time out of Joint* (1959), *The Man in the High Castle* (1962; Hugo Award winner), and *The Three Stigmata of Palmer Eldritch* (1965), the protagonists must determine their own orientation in an "alternate world." In works such as *The Simulacra* (1964) and *Do Androids Dream of Electric Sheep?* (1968; adapted for film as *Blade Runner* [1982]), artificial creatures grapple with what is authentic in a real world of the future.

Among Dick's numerous story collections were *A Handful of Darkness* (1955), *The Variable Man and Other Stories* (1957), *The Preserving Machine* (1969), and *I Hope I Shall Arrive Soon* (published posthumously, 1985). Several of his short stories and novels have been adapted for film, including "We Can Remember It for You Wholesale" (filmed as *Total Recall* [1990 and 2012]), "Second Variety" (filmed as *Screamers* [1995]), "The Minority Report" (filmed as *Minority Report* [2002]), *A Scanner Darkly* (1977; film 2006), and "Adjustment Team" (filmed as *The Adjustment Bureau* [2011]).

Dick endured years of drug abuse and mental illness before dying of heart failure on March 2, 1982, in Santa Ana, California. At that time his reputation was mostly limited to science-fiction circles. By the 21st century, however, he was widely regarded as a master of imaginative, paranoid fiction in the vein of Franz Kafka and Thomas Pynchon.

# CHARLES DICKENS

(b. 1812—d. 1870)

No English author of the 19th century was more popular than the novelist Charles Dickens. With a reporter's eye for the details of daily life, a fine ear for the subtleties of common speech, and unmatched powers of character creation, Dickens created a body of work that brought him worldwide fame. He was a remarkably entertaining comic writer, but he was also much more. His perceptive and compassionate depiction of society and its shortcomings made him an influential advocate for social reform.

Dickens was praised in his lifetime, and his critical reputation has only grown since his death. He is generally considered the greatest writer of the Victorian era, and some critics place him second only to William Shakespeare in all of English literature.

Charles John Huffam Dickens was born on February 7, 1812, in Portsmouth, England. He was the second of eight children. His father, John Dickens, was a clerk in a navy office, a job that required him to move his family frequently. In 1817 the family settled in the town of Chatham, southeast of London, where Charles attended school and developed an interest in English novels of the 18th century. These years in Chatham, which lasted until the family moved to London in 1822, were the happiest of Dickens's childhood. The area would appear often in his novels.

John Dickens earned enough to provide a middle-class lifestyle for his family, but he was a habitually poor manager of money. In 1824 he was sent with his family to the Marshalsea Prison for debt. Charles, the eldest son, did not go to prison, but he was pulled from school and put to work in a factory. Feeling lonely and abandoned, he lived alone in a garret and visited his family in prison on Sundays. Then a timely inheritance restored the family to something like comfortable means, and Charles had a few quiet years at a private school in London.

This period had a lasting impact on Dickens's character and his art. His family's financial troubles and his unpleasant experience with factory life gave Charles a sympathetic knowledge of the lives and trials of

Charles Dickens.

the working class that would inform his writings. Images of prisons and of lost, oppressed children also would recur in his novels. Dickens dramatized some of the liveliness and failings of his father, for whom he always had a great love, as the character Mr. Micawber in the partly autobiographical novel *David Copperfield*. Dickens's mother, unsympathetic and unconscious of his potential, meant less to him; she begrudged his leaving work to return to school. She would become the model for the character Mrs. Nickleby in *Nicholas Nickleby*.

Dickens finished his schooling at age 15 and went to work. He became a clerk in a law office and then, after learning shorthand, a reporter in the law courts and in the House of Commons. In 1834 he joined the staff of the *Morning Chronicle*, for which he traveled to other cities and towns to report election speeches. These jobs gave Dickens a lasting affection for journalism and also an enduring dislike of both law and politics that would be reflected in his novels.

Another influential event of this period was his rejection as suitor to Maria Beadnell, a banker's daughter, because his family and prospects were unsatisfactory. The pain he felt upon losing her sharpened his determination to succeed.

Dickens's first attempt at creative writing grew out of his experience as a journalist. In 1833 he began contributing stories and descriptive essays to magazines and newspapers under the name of Boz, the family nickname of a younger brother. These were collected and in February 1836 reprinted as *Sketches by "Boz,"* which was well received.

That same month the publishers Chapman and Hall asked Dickens to write stories to accompany a monthly series of comic illustrations by a noted artist. Originally the stories and illustrations were to deal with a group of Londoners in a hunting and fishing club, but Dickens, knowing little of the subject, suggested changing the focus to travel. The publishers agreed, and Dickens went on to create Mr. Pickwick, one of the greatest characters in humorous literature. Within a few months the *Pickwick Papers* had made Dickens the most popular author of the day.

The success of *Pickwick* led to new projects that kept Dickens occupied for the next several years. In 1836 he resigned from his newspaper job and became editor of a new monthly magazine, *Bentley's Miscellany*, in which he serialized the novel *Oliver Twist* (1837–39). His other serialized novels of this period were *Nicholas Nickleby* (1838–39), *The Old Curiosity Shop* (1840–41), and *Barnaby Rudge* (1841). Apart from writing, his growing family was another commitment. In April 1836, in the week that the first installment of the *Pickwick Papers* appeared, Dickens married Catherine Hogarth, the daughter of a newspaper associate. The first of their 10 children was born in 1837.

Dickens's novels following the comic *Pickwick Papers* introduced a more serious element that would remain prominent throughout his fiction—attacks on social evils and inadequate institutions. Though still containing much comedy, *Oliver Twist* focused more on exposing the evils of the workhouse and the criminal world through the dramatic story of an orphan. *Nicholas Nickleby* continued in this vein with its criticism of the brutal Yorkshire school system. *The Old Curiosity Shop* is best known for the death of the saintly but suffering Little Nell, a scene considered overwhelmingly powerful at the time but later scorned for its sentimentality. *Barnaby Rudge* was a historical novel set in the late 18th century that dealt with the spectacle of large-scale mob violence.

Exhausted by his intense work schedule, Dickens set out for a five-month vacation to the United States in early 1842. The United States had welcomed his books from the start, in part because the lack of international copyright permitted American publishers to print them without paying him. Dickens, at that stage of his life a radical who hated Toryism and aristocracy, wished to study the United States and its democratic ideals firsthand.

Dickens and his wife sailed to Boston in January 1842, leaving their four children at home. Treated as a literary celebrity, he received an enthusiastic welcome from the New England elite. From Boston he went to New York City, Philadelphia, Washington, D.C., and Richmond, Virginia. Dickens reveled in his adoring audience and wrote home of the freedom of the United States and the comforts of the workers. He traveled westward as far as Missouri before returning to England in June 1842.

Dickens spoke everywhere of the need for an international copyright agreement that would protect the rights of both American and British writers. He felt that it was unfair and unjust that American publishers could print and sell his books without permission from him and without paying him any royalties. Dickens did not speak of himself as the sole victim of this practice. He pointed out that all British authors were equally victimized; he also acknowledged that American authors, such as Edgar Allan Poe, suffered from the pirating of their works in England.

American newspapers attacked these statements and accused Dickens of bad taste and of abusing American hospitality. In time Dickens's rosy view of the United States faded. He was disgusted by slavery, government corruption, and what he saw as the materialism and vulgarity of American life. His disillusionment with the United States is revealed in his nonfiction book *American Notes* (1842) and in the novel *Martin Chuzzlewit* (1843–44).

A shortcoming of Dickens's early novels, as popular as they were, was a lack of narrative unity. Creating a coherent story while writing in monthly, or even weekly, serial installments was a difficult task. In the preface to *Martin Chuzzlewit*, Dickens wrote of his intention "to keep a steadier eye upon the general purpose and design."

Dickens practiced his narrative concentration in a new, shorter type of story that was not serialized—his Christmas books. The first of these, *A Christmas Carol*, was conceived and written in a few weeks in 1843. It became the most enduring Christmas myth of modern literature. Further Christmas books, essays, and stories followed annually (except in 1847) through 1867, but none equaled the *Carol* in quality.

Dickens's first novel to display his new maturity as a writer was *Dombey and Son* (1846–48). Although serialized, this novel was clearly a product of more thorough planning. It also presented a broader criticism of modern society than had his earlier books, which had focused on particular evils. It explored the corruption of money, finding virtue and human decency most often among the poor and humble.

Social concerns are minimal in Dickens's next novel, *David Copperfield* (1849–50), which shows the author at the height of his powers. Written in the first person, it is perhaps most notable for its childhood chapters, which are partly based on Dickens's own experiences. Largely for these reasons, it has always been among his most popular novels. Dickens himself described it as his "favourite child."

Despite his great success as a novelist, Dickens did not wish to limit himself to book writing. His journalism background, his political beliefs, and his desire to secure a steady income independent of his creative writing made him attempt or plan several periodical ventures in the 1840s and 1850s. In 1846 he became editor of the newly founded liberal newspaper the *Daily News*, but within weeks he decided that he was not suited for the job and resigned. In 1850 he finally achieved journalistic success with *Household Words*, a weekly journal that he founded and edited. This publication and its successor, *All the Year Round*, were popular collections of fiction, poetry, and essays on a wide range of topics. Dickens contributed several serials of his own, including novels.

Dickens's other activities often reflected the benevolent spirit apparent in his writings. For more than a decade beginning in 1847 he directed a reformatory home for young female delinquents, financed by his wealthy friend Angela Burdett-Coutts. He also gave public speeches on such issues as water pollution and juvenile illiteracy and participated in fund-raising activities.

Dickens's novels of the 1850s were much darker than their predecessors. Lacking the basic optimism that tempered the social criticism of the earlier works, they present an increasingly somber picture of contemporary society. *Bleak House* (1852–53) and *Little Dorrit* (1855–57) attack the injustices of the English legal system, and *Hard Times* (1854) explores the dehumanizing effects of industrialization on workers and communities. The humor in these novels takes the form of harsh satire. Technically, these novels are more coherent than the earlier fiction, with plots that are more fully related to themes.

The dark tone of these novels reflected a decline in Dickens's spirits. He had lost all faith in government and its willingness to deal with social problems such as poverty and hunger, but he also had no alternative to suggest. At the same time his marriage began to unravel. In 1858 he separated from his wife and began a long affair with Ellen Ternan, a young actress. Fearing the effect of a scandal on his career, Dickens managed to keep the relationship from the public.

Dickens sought relief from the difficulties of his personal life in his work. In the mid-1850s he acted in a number of amateur theatricals to earn money for charity. This carried on his long attraction to the stage, which had almost led him to become a professional actor in the early 1830s. It was on the set of one of these productions, *The Frozen Deep*, that

Dickens met Ellen Ternan in August 1857.

Around the time of his separation from his wife, Dickens began devoting much of his time to public readings from his novels. His emotional involvement in these readings was intense. He felt a close relationship with the public and greatly valued its affection, which served as a substitute for the love he could not find at home.

Dickens began his reading tour in April 1858. The early readings consisted entirely of Christmas books, but he soon added episodes from the novels and magazine Christmas stories. The performances drew on his talent for acting, his love of theatricals and of seeing and delighting an audience, and the dramatic nature of his fiction. He made a number of successful tours in England, Scotland, and Ireland—from 1858 to 1859, 1861 to 1863, 1866 to 1867, and 1869 to 1870. A triumphant American tour in 1867–68 wiped out the bad memories of his earlier trip to the United States.

Dickens greatly enjoyed his readings until, near the end, he was becoming ill and exhausted. He wrote much less in the 1860s, but he remained inventive. *A Tale of Two Cities* (1859), set during the French Revolution, was his first historical novel since *Barnaby Rudge*. It relied less on characterization, dialogue, and humor, but nevertheless it continues to be one of his most popular novels. *Great Expectations* (1860–61) resembles *David Copperfield* in being a first-person narration and in drawing on parts of Dickens's personality and experience. A great critical and popular success, it is perhaps his finest novel. *Our Mutual Friend* (1864–65) continued his ongoing critique of wealth and class values.

Dickens gave his final public reading in London in March 1870. Thereafter he worked on his last novel, *The Mystery of Edwin Drood*, at Gad's Hill, his country house near his boyhood home in Chatham. Dickens died at home on June 9, 1870, leaving the book unfinished. He was buried in Westminster Abbey in London.

# EMILY DICKINSON

(b. 1830—d. 1886)

A New England writer whose work was unknown in her lifetime, Emily Dickinson is regarded today as one of the finest American poets. Although Dickinson's life was uneventful, she enjoyed a full and exciting existence in her imagination. Her poetry is concise and characterized by unusual rhythms and rhymes. Through intimate, domestic figures of speech, it examines topics such as love, death, and nature. Along with Walt Whitman, Dickinson is widely considered to be one of the two leading 19th-century American poets.

Emily Elizabeth Dickinson was born on December 10, 1830, in Amherst, Massachusetts. Her father, Edward Dickinson, was a lawyer and leading citizen of Amherst. Her mother was Emily Norcross Dickinson. Emily had an older brother, William Austin, and a younger sister, Lavinia.

Emily Dickinson, 1848.

Dickinson had more formal education than most women of her time. She attended public schools and the Amherst Academy and spent one year at Mount Holyoke Female Seminary in South Hadley.

Strongly influenced by the work of Ralph Waldo Emerson and Emily Brontë, Dickinson began writing poetry around 1850. In 1855 Dickinson, with her mother and sister, went to Washington, D.C., where her father was in Congress. On their return they stopped in Philadelphia, Pennsylvania, where they met the well-known Reverend Charles Wadsworth.

Dickinson was immediately taken with the brooding, eloquent preacher. Many scholars believe that Wadsworth was the subject of her love poems, the "atom I prefer to all the lists of clay." He was married, however, and the relationship was limited to correspondence and occasional visits by Wadsworth to her family home. In 1861 he was transferred to San Francisco, California.

Dickinson spent the rest of her life quietly at home, writing exhaustively—during the American Civil War period alone she produced some 800 poems. She also corresponded regularly with several people, most of them literary figures and editors.

By 1870, Dickinson's poetic output had slowed. She seldom left her room, appearing occasionally, in a white dress, when guests visited downstairs. Her poetry, which she had shown to few people, remained largely undiscovered—only seven poems were published in her lifetime.

After Dickinson died on May 15, 1886, her sister found her poems. Many were published, extensively edited, in various collections from 1890 to 1925. Not until 1955, however, were all her poems published. They appeared, unedited, in the three-volume *Poems of Emily Dickinson*. The collection *Letters of Emily Dickinson* was published in 1958.

# JOAN DIDION

(b. 1934—d. )

Joan Didion is an American novelist and essayist known for her lucid prose style and incisive depictions of social unrest and psychological fragmentation.

Didion graduated from the University of California, Berkeley, in 1956 and then worked for *Vogue* magazine from 1956 to 1963, first as a copywriter and later as an editor. During this period she wrote her first novel, *Run River* (1963), which examines the disintegration of a California family. While in New York City, she met and married writer John Gregory

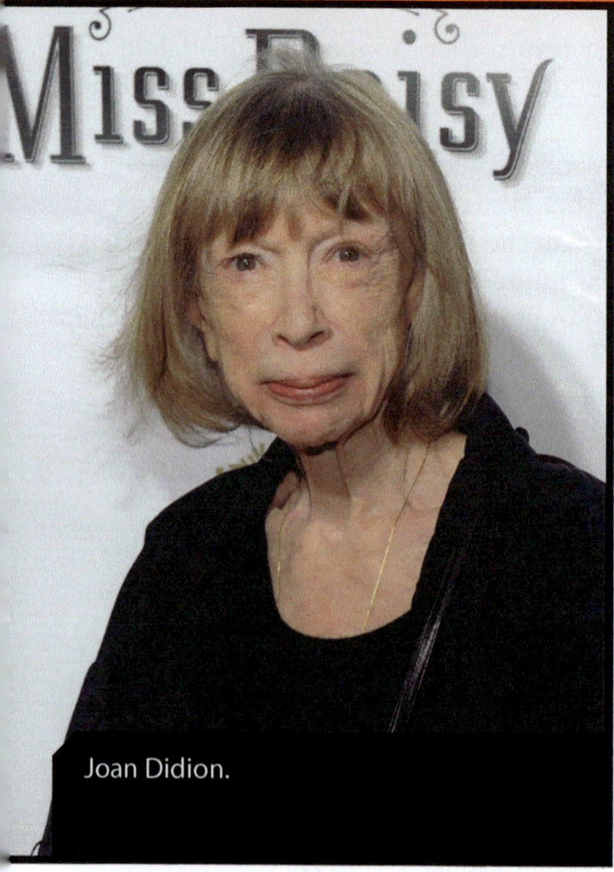


Joan Didion.

Dunne, with whom she returned to California in 1964. A collection of magazine columns published as *Slouching Towards Bethlehem* (1968) established Didion's reputation as an essayist and confirmed her preoccupation with the forces of disorder. In a second collection, *The White Album* (1979), Didion continued her analysis of the turbulent 1960s. The inner decay of the establishment is a major theme of the essays constituting the volume *After Henry* (1992; also published as *Sentimental Journeys*).

Other works by Didion include the short novels *Play It as It Lays* (1970), *A Book of Common Prayer* (1977), *Democracy* (1984), and *The Last Thing He Wanted* (1996) and the essays *Salvador* (1983), *Miami* (1987), and *Where I Was From* (2003). Essays on U.S. politics, including the presidential election of 2000, were collected in *Political Fictions* (2001). Didion also wrote several screenplays with her husband, including *A Star Is Born* (1976; with others), *True Confessions* (1981), and *Up Close and Personal* (1996). Following Dunne's death in 2003, she wrote *The Year of Magical Thinking* (2005), in which she recounted their marriage and mourned his loss. The memoir won a National Book Award, and Didion adapted it for the stage in 2007. In 2011 she again visited tragedy and loss in *Blue Nights*, a memoir in which she attempts to come to terms with the death of her daughter. Didion was honored with the National Humanities Medal in 2013.

# Arthur Conan Doyle

(b. 1859—d. 1930)

A Scottish physician who turned to writing, Arthur Conan Doyle thought he would be remembered for his historical novels. His fame, however, rests on his creation of the master detective of fiction, the incomparable Sherlock Holmes.

Arthur Conan Doyle was born in Edinburgh, Scotland, on May 22, 1859. He was the oldest son of Charles Doyle, a civil servant. His parents were Irish Roman Catholics, and he received his early education in a Jesuit school, Stonyhurst. Later he got a medical degree at Edinburgh University. He started practice as a family physician in Southsea, England. His income was small so he began writing stories to make ends meet. In 1891 he decided to give up medicine to concentrate on his writing.

"A Study in Scarlet," published in 1887, introduced Holmes and his friend Dr. John Watson. The second Holmes story was "The Sign of Four" (1890). In 1891 Doyle began a series for *Strand* magazine called "The Adventures of Sherlock Holmes."

Sherlock Holmes became known to movie and television audiences as a tall and lean, pipe-smoking, violin-playing detective. He lived at 221B Baker Street in London, where he was often visited by Watson, an associate in the many adventures. And according to Doyle, it was Watson who recorded the Holmes stories for posterity.

Doyle said he modeled Holmes after one of his teachers in Edinburgh, Dr. Joseph Bell. Bell could, for example, glance at a corpse on the anatomy table and deduce that the person had been a left-handed shoemaker. "It is all very well to say that a man is clever," Doyle wrote, "but the reader wants to see examples of it—such examples as Bell gave us every day in the wards." The author eventually became bored with Holmes and "killed" him. In response to readers' protests, Doyle wrote his next story explaining how the detective had miraculously survived the death struggle on the edge of a precipice. Stories dealing with Holmes's exploits continued to appear almost to the end of Doyle's life.

Doyle was knighted in 1902 for his pamphlet justifying England's part in the Boer War, in which he served at a field hospital. He was married twice. The death of his son Kingsley in World War I intensified Doyle's interest in psychic phenomena; in his later years he wrote and lectured on spiritualism. He died in Sussex on July 7, 1930.

## GEORGE ELIOT

(b. 1819—d. 1880)

One of England's foremost novelists of the 19th century was Mary Ann (or Marian) Evans, who wrote under the pen name George Eliot. In such novels as *Silas Marner* and *The Mill on the Floss*, Eliot created realistic pictures of English country life. *Middlemarch*, her masterpiece, skillfully depicts every class of society in a provincial town. Eliot wrote with a psychological depth that would become characteristic of modern fiction.

Mary Ann Evans was born in Warwickshire, England, on November 22, 1819. She spent her first years on an estate where her father worked. At age 7 she was sent to boarding school, where she received a strongly Christian education. Mary Ann's mother died when the girl was 16. In 1841 Mary Ann moved with her father to nearby Coventry.

There Marian (as she began writing her name) became a close friend of Charles Bray and his family. Bray, a prosperous manufacturer, had forsaken conventional Christianity in favor of his own system of ethics. Bray's ideas greatly influenced the girl, much to her father's anguish. During these years she translated David Friedrich Strauss's *Life of Jesus Critically Examined* from the original German.

After her father's death in 1849, Marian lived with the Brays. In 1851 she took a job in London as assistant editor of the Westminster Review. She often worked 18 hours a day, but she still found time for social life with the leading writers and thinkers of the day. Among them was George Henry Lewes, a fairly well-known but not very successful journalist. Lewes's wife had deserted him, leaving him their three young sons. In 1854 Marian became his common-law wife in a union that lasted until his death.

George Eliot.

Lewes soon recognized Marian's growing genius and urged her to try fiction. Her first effort was a short story, "The Sad Fortunes of the Reverend Amos Barton." It was accepted by *Blackwood's Magazine* for the January 1857 issue. Marian used her masculine pen name, which she chose to evade prejudice against women writers. For some years no one but Lewes knew who George Eliot was. *Blackwood's* accepted several more stories and reprinted them in a book, *Scenes of Clerical Life*, published in 1858.

For the next 20 years each new book by George Eliot was acclaimed by the critics and widely read by the public. She published *Adam Bede* in 1859; *The Mill on the Floss* (1860); *Silas Marner* (1861); *Romola* (1862–63); *Felix Holt the Radical* (1866); *The Spanish Gypsy* (1868), a dramatic poem; *Brother and Sister* (1869), a sonnet sequence; *Middlemarch* (1871–72); *Daniel Deronda* (1876); and *Impressions of Theophrastus Such* (1879). Income from the books enabled George Eliot and Lewes to live fashionably, to entertain, and to travel.

Their happy life together ended with Lewes's death in 1878. George Eliot wrote no more, and for a long time she mourned him deeply. In 1880 she married John W. Cross, a friend of many years. Only a few months later, on December 22, 1880, she died. Cross arranged her letters and journals into *Life*, published in 1885. This has been the main source for succeeding biographies.

# RALPH ELLISON

(b. 1914—d. 1994)

For seven years Ralph Ellison poured both his firsthand awareness of the plight of African Americans and his belief in the United States as a land of possibility into the novel that became *Invisible Man*. On the basis of that single work, published in 1952, Ellison established his reputation as a major 20th-century American writer.

Ralph Waldo Ellison was born in Oklahoma City, Oklahoma, on March 1, 1914. He was named after Ralph Waldo Emerson, the 19th-century essayist, by his father, a construction worker and avid reader. As a boy he was interested in music and reading, and at age 8 he began to play the trumpet. Later he studied classical music at Tuskegee Institute.

In 1936 Ellison visited New York City to study sculpture and to work in the Federal Writers' Project. There he met the African American authors Langston Hughes and Richard Wright, who inspired him to become a writer. In 1937 Ellison moved to New York City, and he was soon contributing essays, short stories, and articles to several publications.

After serving in World War II, Ellison wrote *Invisible Man*, which won the 1953 National Book Award for fiction. In a complex and symbolic narrative, the partly autobiographical novel relates one African American's struggle to find his place in a racially divided society while simultaneously exploring the universal human search for identity. Like the novel, many of Ellison's short stories explore the relationship of African Americans to their heritage and the place of blacks in white society. Ellison's other full-length works, *Shadow and Act* (1964) and *Going to the Territory* (1986), were collections of essays and interviews.

Ellison lectured widely on African American culture, folklore, and creative writing and taught at several U.S. colleges and universities. After a fire destroyed much of the manuscript of a second novel in 1967, Ellison spent the remaining years of his life painstakingly attempting to re-create his work. The project was left unfinished at his death on April 16, 1994, in New York City. In 1999 an edition of the novel was published by his literary executor, John Callahan, with the title *Juneteenth*.

# RALPH WALDO EMERSON

(b. 1803—d. 1882)

The writings of Ralph Waldo Emerson, perhaps the most inspirational writer in American literature, had a powerful influence on his generation. They have also stood the test of time.

Emerson was born in Boston on May 25, 1803. When he was 8 years old, his father, who was pastor of the First Church in Boston, died. His mother took in boarders to support the family of six children.

His education began early. Before he was 3, his father had complained that he did not yet read very well. He entered Harvard College when he was 14. He graduated at 18 but received no honors because he preferred to read what he pleased rather than the lessons assigned to him.

After leaving Harvard, Emerson taught school for three years. This gave him enough money to enter the divinity school at Harvard. In 1826 he began to preach. In 1829 he was ordained and was appointed minister of a large Unitarian church in Boston. In the same year he married Ellen Louisa Tucker. Emerson at this time was quiet, retiring, and self-contained. He thought much, wrote a little, and said less. He was genial toward the people around him, but he was difficult to know intimately.

When he was 28, Emerson began to experience his darkest years. His wife died in 1831 at the age of 19. Her death was soon followed by those of Emerson's brilliant brothers, Edward and Charles. Emerson's health broke. He suffered also from doubts about church doctrine and felt that he could no longer administer the Lord's Supper. In 1832 he resigned his pastorate, explaining, "It is my desire to do nothing which I cannot do with my whole heart."

He then sailed for Europe. In England he met most of the great intellectuals of the day, including William Wordsworth, Samuel Taylor Coleridge, John Stuart Mill, and, above all, Thomas Carlyle, whom he greatly admired. But travel and even the famous people he met seemed to mean little to Emerson. He said in his essay *Nature*, published some years later: "The difference between landscape and landscape is small, but there is a great difference in the beholder." As for his acquaintances, they seemed to him inferior in intellect, except Carlyle, with whom he corresponded for many years.

When Emerson returned to the United States in 1833, he had begun to lecture and to write freely. He helped launch the *Dial*, an important literary magazine, in 1840 and later edited it for a few years. Harvard asked him to give several addresses, one of which, "The American Scholar," was called by Oliver Wendell Holmes "our intellectual Declaration of Independence."

Emerson married Lydia Jackson in 1835. Previously he had purchased a house with a garden in Concord, Massachusetts, and there, surrounded by his family, he passed the rest of his life except for occasional lecture engagements and two journeys to Europe. When his house burned in

1872, a nationwide popular subscription was taken and the funds used to rebuild it. He died after a short illness on April 27, 1882, and was buried in Sleepy Hollow Cemetery.

To understand Emerson's aloofness from people and events, it is necessary to understand his way of thinking. He believed that great truths come by intuition—that is, that they come unbidden. Furious striving avails nothing; truth comes gently. Most modern philosophers do not agree with Emerson; they think that truth may be reasoned.

How are people to arrive at truth? Emerson gives his answer in his essay "Self Reliance": "To believe your own thought, to believe that what is true for you in your private heart is true for all men—that is genius. Speak your latent conviction and it shall be the universal sense; for always the inmost becomes the outmost—and our first thought is rendered back to us by the trumpets of the last judgment." "God is in every man." The last phrase is the keynote of what is called Transcendentalism, or that faith in the inner light of which Emerson was the chief exponent.

There was something more than truth that drew the crowds to Emerson's lectures, something that still holds all those who turn to Emerson for enlightenment. In the early days people often came to scoff and remained to listen, much impressed. Emerson the man held them. He was a man of charm and vigor; he had a style almost without equal.

Oliver Wendell Holmes said: "No one who ever heard him speak will forget the play of his features, the lighting up of his eyes with a rapt inner illumination, the emphatic stamp of his foot when some weighty thought required enforcement." In the matter of style he stands supreme for his power of saying much in little, of so phrasing his thoughts that they sparkle and glow. Every sentence seems as good as the one it follows. This is true of his poetry as well as his prose; in both he showed the power of stating truth in sharp relief. His poems are ranked among the greatest ever written in the United States.

Emerson's principal works are *Nature*, published in 1836; *Essays, First Series* (1841); *Essays, Second Series* (1844); *Representative Men* (1850); *English Traits* (1856); *The Conduct of Life* (1860); and *Society and Solitude* (1870). His poetry was published in the volumes *Poems* (1847) and *May-Day* (1867). Emerson has been criticized for the lack of organization or plan in his essays, but these were not his primary concerns. He said what he had to say as it came to him and considered himself as the mouthpiece. Emerson is still read—while many of his critics have long been forgotten.

## WILLIAM FAULKNER

(b. 1897—d. 1962)

The novels of American author William Faulkner rank among the most important books of the 20th century. For them he was awarded the 1949 Nobel Prize in Literature. Faulkner wrote mostly about his hometown of Oxford, in Lafayette County, Mississippi. In his fiction the place was renamed Jefferson, in Yoknapatawpha County. The time in various stories ranges from pre-Civil War days to the early 1960s. People of all sorts—wealthy and poor, evil and good, slave and free—come into sharp focus in his writing.

William Cuthbert Falkner (he later changed the spelling of his last name to Faulkner) was born on September 25, 1897, in New Albany, Mississippi. Early in his childhood the family moved to Oxford, Mississippi, where his father later became business manager of the University of Mississippi. William left high school before graduating. He did, however, read widely, and he was well aware of his family background, especially that of his great-grandfather, who had fought in the American Civil War, built a railroad, and written a popular romantic novel, *The White Rose of Memphis*.

In mid-1918, Faulkner joined the British Royal Air Force as a cadet pilot under training in Canada, but a few months later World War I ended, before his training was even completed. Back home after the war, he took a few courses at the university and began publishing poems and drawings in campus newspapers. In 1924 Faulkner published *The Marble Faun*, a pastoral verse-sequence in rhymed octosyllabic couplets.

After two apprentice novels—*Soldiers' Pay* (1926) and *Mosquitoes* (1927)—Faulkner became chiefly concerned with proving himself as a professional writer. The novel *Sartoris* appeared in 1929. It created in print for the first time the densely imagined world of Jefferson and Yoknapatawpha County. Faulkner's first major novel, *The Sound and the*

*Fury* (1929), combined a Yoknapatawpha setting with a radical technical experimentation called stream of consciousness. In this narrative technique, Faulker used snatches of incoherent thought, ungrammatical constructions, and the free association of ideas and images to record the minds of his characters. He continued his stream-of-consciousness technique in the tragicomedy *As I Lay Dying* (1930). The novel relates the travails of a poor family traveling to bury its matriarch's decaying corpse.

By the early 1930s, Faulkner's budding popularity allowed him to publish short stories in popular magazines such as *Collier's* and *Saturday Evening Post*. He won greater acclaim with the financially successful publication of *Sanctuary* (1931), a novel about the brutal rape of a Southern college student and its generally violent consequences. The long and complexly structured novel *Light in August* (1932) revolves primarily upon the contrasted careers of a pregnant young countrywoman in pursuit of her biological destiny and a dark-complexioned orphan uncertain as to his racial origins. In *Absalom, Absalom!* (1936) the main character arrives in Jefferson from "nowhere," ruthlessly carves a large plantation out of the Mississippi wilderness, and fights valiantly in the Civil War in defense of his adopted society, but is ultimately destroyed by his inhumanity toward those whom he has used and cast aside in the obsessive pursuit of his grandiose dynastic "design."

Later works of Faulkner include his trilogy about the Snopes family, which includes *The Hamlet* (1940), *The Town* (1957), and *The Mansion* (1959). *Go Down, Moses* (1942) explores the linked themes of racial, sexual, and environmental exploitation in terms of the complex interactions between the "white" and "black" branches of a plantation-owning family; *Intruder in the Dust* (1948) revisits a character from *Go Down, Moses*. Two collections of Faulkner's work—*The Portable Faulkner* (1946) and *Collected Stories* (1950)—were well-received. After Faulkner was awarded the Nobel Prize in Literature, he was catapulted to the peak of world fame. His other accomplishments included Pulitzer Prizes for *A Fable* (1954), a long, densely written, and complexly structured novel about World War I, and *The Reivers* (1962), a nostalgic comedy subtitled *A Reminiscence*. Faulkner died on July 6, 1962, in Byhalia, Mississippi.

# F. SCOTT FITZGERALD

(b. 1896—d. 1940)

The novels and short stories of F. Scott Fitzgerald are famous for portraying the "lost generation" of the post–World War I era. They depict the rich, disenchanted youth of what he called the Jazz Age.

Francis Scott Key Fitzgerald was born in St. Paul, Minnesota, on September 24, 1896, the only son of Edward and Mary Fitzgerald. His father was a descendant of Francis Scott Key, author of 'The Star-Spangled Banner.' Fitzgerald attended St. Paul Academy and the Newman School, in New Jersey. After entering Princeton University in 1913 he wrote for student publications. In November 1917 Fitzgerald left college to enlist in the Army. While stationed in Montgomery, Alabama, he fell in love with Zelda Sayre.

Following his release from the Army in 1919, Fitzgerald worked for an advertising agency in New York City for several months. After Zelda broke their engagement, he returned to St. Paul to rewrite a novel he had worked on when he was in the Army. The novel—*This Side of Paradise*—was published in 1920. The first chronicle of flaming youth, it brought Fitzgerald fame, money, and marriage to Zelda.

To maintain the luxurious life he and his wife liked to lead, Fitzgerald wrote at a furious pace. In 1920 he published *Flappers and Philosophers*, a volume of short stories. His second novel, *The Beautiful and Damned*, and *Tales of the Jazz Age* appeared in 1922. In 1924 the Fitzgeralds moved to Europe, where Fitzgerald wrote his masterpiece, *The Great Gatsby*. Typical of his work, it glorified romance and disillusionment, and the dialogue was flawless.

In 1930 Zelda suffered a breakdown, a step on the way to her insanity. The family returned to the United States in 1930. Fitzgerald's novel *Tender Is the Night* was published in 1934. It failed to sell, and Fitzgerald felt defeated. In 1936 he wrote about his emotional state in *The Crack-up*.

Fitzgerald went to Hollywood in 1937 to write scenarios for motion pictures. On December 20, 1940, he suffered a fatal heart attack. He had begun a novel about Hollywood, called *The Last Tycoon*. The unfinished

F. Scott Fitzgerald.

work, published in 1941, was another attempt to create his dream of the promises of American life and of a man who could realize them.

# GUSTAVE FLAUBERT

(b. 1821—d. 1880)

Writing was not easy for the French novelist Gustave Flaubert. Because of his concern for form and precise detail, he often struggled for days searching for *le seul mot juste* ("the exactly right word"). He took five years to write *Madame Bovary*, his best-known work.

Gustave Flaubert was born on December 12, 1821, in Rouen, France, where his father, Achille, was chief surgeon at the Hôtel-Dieu (hospital). His mother, Caroline Fleuriot, was the daughter of a doctor. Gustave was one of six children, only three of whom survived.

While a student in Rouen, Gustave showed an early interest in literature. He and his friends acted in plays he had written when he was only 11. His first published work, *Song of Death*, appeared in the review *Le Colibri* in 1837.

At the insistence of his father, Flaubert went to Paris in 1841 to study law. In 1843, having failed his examinations and suffering from the onset of a nervous disorder, he decided to devote all his time to literature. After the deaths of his father and sister, in 1846, a sizable inheritance enabled him to retire to the family estate at Croisset to write.

Flaubert sought to make literature a pure art. His aim was to write faultless, meticulously chiseled prose. "My head reels and throat aches with chasing after, slogging over, delving into, turning around, groping after, and bellowing, in a hundred thousand different ways, a sentence that I've at last finished," he said while working on *Madame Bovary*. In this novel, which tells of Emma Bovary's revolt against her middle-class environment, Flaubert reveals his own contempt for the bourgeoisie. This group, he felt, was opposed to art and hated everything that it could not put to use.

When *Madame Bovary* first appeared—in 1856, as a magazine serial—Flaubert was brought to trial for publishing a morally offensive work. He was acquitted in 1857, and in the same year the novel came out in book form.

During his later years, Flaubert spent the winter in Paris, where he held literary gatherings. One of his guests was the writer Guy de Maupassant, whom he tutored for ten years.

Flaubert never married. He devoted most of his life to caring for his mother and his niece. In 1875 he gave his fortune to save the niece's husband from bankruptcy. Flaubert died on May 8, 1880, at Croisset.

Among Flaubert's other works are the novels *Salammbô* (published in 1862), *L'Education sentimentale* (*Sentimental Education*, 1869), and *La Tentation de St. Antoine* (*The Temptation of St. Anthony*, 1874). There are also a book of short stories, *Trois Contes* (Three Tales, 1877), and letters.

# E.M. FORSTER

(b. 1879—d. 1970)

The works of the English novelist E.M. Forster have their roots in the Romantic movement: they urge humanity to maintain a close relationship with nature and, at the same time, to develop the imagination. These themes, albeit in a negative way, run through his best-known book, *A Passage to India* (1924; film, 1984), and they were expressed in a more positive way in his earlier novels, *The Longest Journey* (1907) and *Howards End* (1910; film, 1992).

Edward Morgan Forster was born in London on January 1, 1879. He attended Tonbridge School at Kent and King's College, Cambridge. Upon leaving school, he decided to devote himself to writing. His early works, written in a plainer and more colloquial style than had been common in the 19th century, were filled with social commentary and criticisms of middle-class life in England, but they also gave indication of the deeper Romantic inclinations that dominated his later novels and short stories. Much of the inspiration for his writing came from travel, particularly in the Mediterranean area and India.

Forster's other novels include *Where Angels Fear to Tread* (1905) and *A Room with a View* (1908; film 1986). Among his nonfiction works are

*Alexandria: A History and a Guide* (1922; new edition, 1961), *Aspects of the Novel* (1927), *Two Cheers for Democracy* (1951), and *The Hill of Devi* (1953). He died in Coventry, England, on June 7, 1970.

# ROBERT FROST

(b. 1874—d. 1963)

The works of U.S. poet Robert Frost tell of simple things—swinging on a birch tree, stopping by woods on a snowy evening, the death of a hired man. Behind them is a deep feeling for life's fundamentals—love, loyalty, awareness of nature and of God.

Frost was born on March 26, 1874, in San Francisco. His father, a newspaper editor, died when Robert was 11. The boy and his mother went to live with his grandfather in Lawrence, Massachusetts. In high school Frost was covaledictorian with Elinor White, whom he married in 1895.

Although Frost sold his first poem in 1894, he was not able to earn a living as a poet until more than 20 years later. He attended Dartmouth College for a few months in 1892, then tried teaching, reporting, and other work. After he married he studied at Harvard University for two years. In 1900 his grandfather gave him a small farm near Derry, New Hampshire. He worked the land unsuccessfully for 11 years, supplementing his income by teaching. The walks that he took on his farm allowed him to discover the beginnings of new poems. From 1912 to 1915 the Frosts lived in England. There were published the two collections that at last brought Frost recognition: *A Boy's Will*, published in 1913, and *North of Boston* (1914).

Honors followed over the years, including Pulitzer Prizes in 1924 for *New Hampshire* (1923), in 1931 for *Collected Poems* (1930), in 1937 for *A Further Range* (1936), and in 1943 for *A Witness Tree* (1942). Among his other books were *Mountain Interval* (1916), *West-Running Brook* (1928), and *In the Clearing* (1962).

Frost taught or held advisory posts at Amherst and Dartmouth colleges, the University of Michigan, Harvard University, and other schools.

He was a cofounder of the Bread Loaf School of English of Middlebury College in Vermont. In his later years, he earned many more honors and awards. He was the poetry consultant to the Library of Congress—the post now called poet laureate consultant—from 1958 to 1959, and he received the Congressional Gold Medal in 1960. He was invited to recite his poem "The Gift Outright" at the inauguration of U.S. President John F. Kennedy in 1961. Frost died in Boston on January 29, 1963.

## GABRIEL GARCÍA MÁRQUEZ

(b. 1927—d. 2014)

Few authors have achieved so successful a blending of comedy, pathos, myth, fantasy, and ironic satire as Gabriel García Márquez. His supreme work, the novel *One Hundred Years of Solitude*, published in 1967, recounts the history of the fictional Colombian village of Macondo and its founders. García Márquez was awarded the Nobel Prize in Literature in 1982.

Gabriel García Márquez, 1982.

García Márquez was born in Aracataca, Colombia, on March 6, 1927. Although he studied law at the National University of Colombia in Bogotá and at the University of Cartagena, he became a journalist, the trade at which he earned his living before attaining literary fame. García Márquez worked on newspapers in Colombia and served as foreign correspondent for Bogotá's daily *El Espectador* in Rome and Paris. From 1959 to 1961 he worked for the Cuban news agency Prensa Latina in Bogotá, Havana, and New York City. Later he moved to Mexico City, where he wrote *One Hundred Years of Solitude*. From 1967 to 1975, he lived in Spain. Subsequently, he kept a house in Mexico City and an apartment in Paris, but he also spent much time in Cuba and Colombia.

García Márquez began writing fiction in the late 1940s. In his first novel, *The Leaf Storm* (1955), he created Macondo, the setting of many later works, and originated his style of magic realism. He next published the novella *No One Writes to the Colonel* (1961), the novel *In Evil Hour* (1962), and his first short-story collection, *Big Mama's Funeral* (1962). Later works include the novels *The Autumn of the Patriarch* (1975), *Chronicle of a Death Foretold* (1981), *Love in the Time of Cholera* (1985), *The General in His Labyrinth* (1989), and *Memories of My Melancholy Whores* (2004).

Among García Márquez's numerous works of nonfiction were *News of a Kidnapping* (1996), a journalistic chronicle of drug-related kidnappings in Colombia, and the memoir *Living to Tell the Tale* (2002). The latter work, written after he was diagnosed with cancer in 1999, focuses on García Márquez's first 30 years. He died on April 17, 2014, in Mexico City, Mexico.

## JOHANN WOLFGANG VON GOETHE

(b. 1749—d. 1832)

In the ranks of German authors Goethe's standing is comparable to Shakespeare's in English literature. Goethe's personality is revealed everywhere in his writings, and many readers have found Goethe himself to be even more fascinating than the characters he created in his stories and poems.

Goethe was born in Frankfurt am Main, Germany, on August 28, 1749. His father was a lawyer and state councillor. His mother was only 18 when Goethe was born. She once said, "My Wolf and I were children

Johann Wolfgang von Goethe.

together." Goethe inherited his zest for life and his lively imagination from her. From his methodical father he got steadiness of purpose. These two strains of inherited traits helped him find the "golden mean" in his life and in his writing.

Goethe grew up in a time of great political change. The Seven Years' War, from 1756 to 1763, established Prussian power and shook all Europe. For a while the French judge advocate general was quartered in the Goethes' house. Meanwhile, Wolfgang and his sister were taught at home by their father and private tutors. The boy was a good student of literature. He wrote his first plays for a small puppet theater, a gift from his grandmother.

When Goethe was 16 he entered the University of Leipzig as a law student. He completed his studies at the University of Strasbourg and was awarded a doctor of laws degree in 1771. The critic Johann Gottfried von Herder introduced him to old German folktales and to the best of English literature in German translation.

Goethe returned to Frankfurt to practice law but turned to writing almost at once. In 1773 his drama *Götz von Berlichingen* was published; the following year he wrote *The Sorrows of Young Werther*. Both works were strongly influenced by the Sturm und Drang (Storm and Stress) literary movement that was sweeping Germany. *Werther* made Goethe known throughout Europe.

In 1774 Goethe met Karl August, duke of Saxe-Weimar. The duke wanted someone to restore order in his state affairs. Goethe became his minister of state, and for the next 11 years the writer devoted himself to practical problems. He became an expert in the fields of taxation, industrial management, farming, and mining.

During this time Goethe wrote little. He wanted to return to literature so he asked the duke for a release. Although the duke refused, Goethe left for a stay in Italy from 1786 to 1788. Goethe regarded his Italian journey as the most important period in his life. He realized the Sturm und Drang school had gone too far, and in the classic art and architecture of Italy he found the order and restraint that guided his work from then on. He became conservative but never reactionary.

Goethe returned to Weimar to live, but he served the duke only as an adviser. Later he became the director of the duke's court theater.

Because of Goethe, Weimar became the intellectual center of Germany. Many great men came to live in the town. Among them was the poet and dramatist Friedrich Schiller. He and Goethe became close friends and helped each other in their writings. Goethe's fame spread over Europe and to the United States. After meeting him, Napoleon exclaimed, "There is a man!"

Goethe had many romantic attachments, but he did not marry until he was 57. His wife was Christiane Vulpius, whom he met in Rome. She remained apart from Goethe's intellectual life.

Goethe once said that his poems made up a "great confession." In a sense the dramatic poem *Faust* is a "confession" of his whole life. As a child he learned the story from a puppet play; he wrote the last scene of his *Faust* in old age. For most of his life he held the story in his mind until at last it became an expression of his mature thought and philosophy.

The story is simple, but its implications are profound. In Goethe's version *Faust* desires all knowledge. Unsatisfied with the results of his studies, he turns to magic. He conjures the devil in the shape of Mephistopheles and makes an agreement with him. If he can gratify *Faust*'s every wish, *Faust*'s soul will belong to Mephistopheles. *Faust* learns that personal pleasures are not happiness. His wishes reach their highest point in a grand project that will benefit others. The moral height he has reached calls the powers of heaven to his aid. In response they wrest his soul from Mephistopheles's hold.

*Faust* was completed in 1831. Goethe died in Weimar on March 22, 1832. His chief works, in addition to *Faust*, were *Götz von Berlichingen* (1773), *The Sorrows of Young Werther* (1774), *Iphigenie auf Tauris* (1787), *Egmont* (1788), *Torquato Tasso* (1790), *Reynard the Fox* (1793), *Wilhelm Meister's Apprenticeship* (1796), *Hermann and Dorothea* (1797), and *Poetry and Fiction*, an autobiography published in four installments (1811, 1812, 1814, 1833).

# DASHIELL HAMMETT

(b. 1894—d. 1961)

One of Humphrey Bogart's most memorable roles was as private detective Sam Spade in the film version of *The Maltese Falcon*. The movie was based on the novel by mystery writer Dashiell Hammett. Although all of his published works were written within a ten-year period, Hammett probably had more influence on the detective story than any other American author after Edgar Allan Poe. His books were the first and best attempt to render realistically the world of American crime. He created the hard-boiled school of detective fiction, a tradition that was later taken up by Mickey Spillane, Ross Macdonald, and others.

Samuel Dashiell Hammett was born on May 27, 1894, in St. Mary's County, Maryland. At 14 he left school to work at odd jobs for eight years before joining the Pinkerton Detective Agency. He served in World War I, where he contracted tuberculosis, and spent several years afterward in Army hospitals. He began to publish short stories in about 1923 in pulp magazines. His first novels were *Red Harvest* and *The Dain Curse*, both published in 1929. *The Maltese Falcon* came out in 1930 and *The Glass Key* in 1931. In *The Thin Man* (1932), his last book, he created the characters Nick and Nora Charles, a detective couple about whom several movies and a television series were made. Nora was based on his friend, playwright Lillian Hellman. Hammett served in World War II as an enlisted man. He died in New York City on January 10, 1961.

# THOMAS HARDY

(b. 1840—d. 1928)

Essentially a tragic novelist, Thomas Hardy wrote books that strike many readers as overly gloomy and pessimistic. A great novelist of the Victorian era, Hardy was also an accomplished poet.

Hardy was born on June 2, 1840, in Upper Bockhampton, near

Dorchester in Dorsetshire, England. He passed most of his long life in this region of woodland, heath, and moor. It forms the setting of most of his writings, under its old name of Wessex. He attended local schools until he was 16, when he became an apprentice in an architect's office in Dorchester. In 1862 Hardy went to London to work as assistant to an architect. He had already begun to write verse and essays.

Hardy returned to Dorchester in 1867 because of ill health and soon began writing prose fiction for a living. His first really successful novel, published serially in 1874, was *Far from the Madding Crowd*. Others are *Under the Greenwood Tree* (1872), *The Return of the Native* (1878), *Tess of the D'Urbervilles* (1891), and *Jude the Obscure* (1895). His poetry includes *Wessex Poems* (1898) and *Time's Laughing-stocks* (1909). *The Dynasts* (1903–08) is an epic drama in three parts.

Hardy viewed nature as a real power affecting the lives of his characters. His novels are realistic, but they resemble Greek tragedies in the way they show their characters as helpless victims of an unfeeling fate. Hardy's sympathy for his characters, even when they had done wrong, caused some of his works to be condemned as immoral.

In 1874 Hardy married Emma Lavinia Gifford, who died in 1912. In 1914 he married his secretary, Florence Emily Dugdale. He died in Dorchester on January 11, 1928. His ashes were placed in Westminster Abbey, but his heart, at his request, was buried in Stinsford, near his birthplace.

## NATHANIEL HAWTHORNE

(b. 1804—d. 1864)

American novelist and short-story writer Nathaniel Hawthorne was friends with a number of noted Transcendentalists, including Ralph Waldo Emerson, Henry David Thoreau, and Bronson Alcott. Hawthorne's works, however, show little of the optimism and self-confidence that marked Transcendentalism. Instead, he preferred themes drawn more from a Puritan preoccupation with guilt and the natural depravity of humans. A master of the symbolic tale, Hawthorne was one of the greatest fiction writers in American literature. He wrote during the American Renaissance, a flowering of literary works in the United States that formed the basis of a new national literature.

Hawthorne was born on July 4, 1804, in Salem, Massachusetts. His family, early Puritan settlers in America, had lived in Salem since the 1600s. One of his ancestors had been a judge in the Salem witch trials. Hawthorne's father, a ship's captain, died when Nathaniel was only four, and his mother became a virtual recluse. Hawthorne attended Bowdoin College in Brunswick, Maine, where he befriended Franklin Pierce, who later became president of the United States.

While a college student, Hawthorne decided to become a writer. Upon graduation, he wrote an amateurish novel, *Fanshawe*, which he published anonymously at his own expense in 1828. However, he soon began writing impressive and distinctive short stories that were published in magazines. By 1832 "My Kinsman, Major Molineux" and "Roger Malvin's Burial," two of his greatest tales—and among the finest in the English language—had appeared. "Young Goodman Brown," perhaps the greatest tale of witchcraft ever written, appeared in 1835. Some of the stories he had sold to magazines were published as *Twice Told Tales* in 1837. The publication cost of the collection was underwritten by one of his college friends, Horatio Bridge. Hawthorne worked in the Boston Customhouse from 1839 to 1840, after which he spent a few months at Brook Farm, a cooperative agricultural community in West Roxbury, Massachusetts. His Brook Farm experience was later described in his novel *The Blithedale Romance* (1852).

In 1842 Hawthorne married Sophia Peabody. For the next three years the young couple rented the Old Manse, the home of Ralph Waldo Emerson's ancestors in Concord, Massachusetts. There Hawthorne wrote a series of stories that appeared in an expanded edition of *Twice Told Tales* (1842). His *Mosses from an Old Manse*, a short-story collection published in 1846, includes an essay describing the Hawthornes' happy life in Concord. In 1845 Hawthorne returned to Salem and again worked in a customhouse. Relieved of that job in 1849, he found more time to write.

Hawthorne's best-known work, *The Scarlet Letter*, was published in 1850. This novel tells the story of Hester Prynne, a young woman in a

Puritan community who has borne a child out of wedlock. The community forces her to wear the red letter A on her dress in order to shame her for having committed adultery. She and her lover are kept apart by the ironies of fate, their own strengths and weaknesses, and the Puritan community's interpretation of moral law. The book made Hawthorne famous and was eventually recognized as one of the greatest of American novels.

Moving from Salem to Lenox, Massachusetts, Hawthorne wrote *The House of the Seven Gables*, which came out in 1851. The novel is a somber tale about a family living under a curse for generations until the curse is removed by love. At Lenox, Hawthorne made the acquaintance of Herman Melville, a fellow writer whose novels show Hawthorne's influence. After a short stay in West Newton, Massachusetts, the Hawthornes returned to Concord, where they purchased a house that had belonged to Bronson Alcott, renaming it Wayside.

In 1853 Franklin Pierce became president. He offered Hawthorne a consulship in Liverpool, England, a government post that Hawthorne held until 1857. After resigning his position as consul, Hawthorne traveled in Europe, mostly in Italy. In 1860 the Hawthornes returned to their home in Concord. After *The Marble Faun*, published that year, Hawthorne wrote little. He aged rapidly and found it increasingly difficult to write. On May 19, 1864, while traveling with his friend Pierce, Hawthorne died in Plymouth, New Hampshire.

Hawthorne wrote relatively little, but if he had written only *The Scarlet Letter* his position as a major American writer would have been assured. The symbolism, psychological insight, and clarity of expression found in his writing have provided a model for generations of American writers.

# ERNEST HEMINGWAY

(b. 1899—d. 1961)

A writer famous for his terse, direct style, Ernest Hemingway was also known for the way in which his own life mirrored the activities and interests of his characters. Many of his works show man pitted against nature, as in his favorite sports—hunting, fishing, and bullfighting. In others he tells of the experiences of wartime—man against man. The immediate appeal of his best writing probably stems from the fact that he wrote of things he knew intimately and that were important to him.

Ernest Hemingway was born on July 21, 1899, in Oak Park, Illinois, a Chicago suburb. His father was a doctor. After high school Hemingway got a job as a reporter on the *Kansas City Star*. During World War I he tried to enlist in the armed forces but was rejected because of an old eye injury. He volunteered as an ambulance driver on the Italian front, and in 1918 he was badly wounded.

After the war he settled in Paris, France, where he began to write fiction. He submitted his work for criticism to the poet Ezra Pound and to Gertrude Stein, a writer who served as friend and adviser to many writers of the time.

The first of many collections of stories, *In Our Time* published in 1925, did not sell well. His novel *The Sun Also Rises*, which came out a year later, made his name known. It tells of young people in postwar Paris and their search for values in a world that in many ways has lost its meaning.

The writing of books occupied Hemingway for most of the postwar years. He remained based in Paris, but he traveled widely for the skiing, bullfighting, fishing, and hunting that by then had become part of his life and formed the background for much of his writing. His position as a master of short fiction had been advanced by *Men Without Women* in 1927 and thoroughly established with the stories in *Winner Take Nothing* in 1933. Among his finest stories are "The Killers," "The Short Happy Life of Francis Macomber," and "The Snows of Kilimanjaro."

In *A Farewell to Arms* (1929), about war on the Italian front, Hemingway tells a love story that is interspersed with scenes of magnificent battle reporting. *To Have and Have Not* (1937) shows Hemingway's interest in social problems, an interest more fully realized in *For Whom the Bell Tolls* (1940), set in the Spanish Civil War. In *Across the River and into the Trees* (1950) an army officer dies while on leave. This novel is generally considered inferior to *The Old Man and the Sea* (1952), which won a Pulitzer Prize in 1953. Hemingway received the Nobel Prize in Literature in 1954.

Hemingway was a war correspondent in Spain, China, and Europe during World War II. He was married four times and had three sons.

Toward the end of his life he suffered from anxiety and depression. He died on July 2, 1961, at his home in Ketchum, Idaho, of a self-inflicted shotgun wound.

# VICTOR HUGO

(b. 1802—d. 1885)

The great French novelist and poet Victor Hugo created two of the most famous characters in literature—Jean Valjean, the ex-convict hero of *Les Misérables*, and the hunchback Quasimodo in *The Hunchback of Notre Dame*. Known for the vast range and immense quantity of his output, Hugo was able during much of his long life to write as many as 100 lines of verse or 20 pages of prose each day.

Victor-Marie Hugo was born in Besançon on February 26, 1802, the son of an officer in Napoleon's army. Hugo's father and mother did not get along, and most of his early years were spent in Paris, where his mother preferred to live. Hugo and his two brothers knew their father from occasional visits as a grand man in a splendid uniform.

In preparatory school, Hugo began to write. He won poetry prizes and wrote for a literary magazine he helped found. In 1821 the magazine failed. Hugo's mother died the same year. After a period of extreme poverty, Hugo was awarded an annual pension by Louis XVIII for his *Miscellaneous Odes and Poems*, published in 1822. He then married his childhood sweetheart, Adèle Foucher.

Between 1822 and 1832 Hugo established himself as a major literary figure in France. He wrote poetry, novels, and plays and became a leader in the Romantic movement.

In 1830 his play Hernani was a spectacular success. By shattering the artificial rules that had previously governed the writing of French drama, Hugo brought new freedom to the French stage. His novel *Notre Dame de Paris* was published in 1831. Translated as *The Hunchback of Notre Dame*, it became vastly popular in many countries. In 1832 his play *Le Roi s'amuse*, or *The King's Diversion*, on which Giuseppe Verdi later based his opera *Rigoletto*, was staged. Like so many of Hugo's works, *The Hunchback of*

*Notre Dame* and *The King's Diversion* were criticisms of social and political injustice. Another reason for writing the plays was to provide parts for the young actress Juliette Negroni, who became his mistress in 1833 and was to be his companion for the rest of her life.

In 1841 Hugo was elected to the French Academy, and in 1849 he became a member of the National Assembly. An outspoken political opponent of Napoleon III, Hugo had to flee France in 1851.

He remained in exile until 1870. During that time he wrote some of his finest works. In 1862 appeared *Les Misérables*, one of the most popular novels of all time. Hugo's wife died in 1868, and Negroni moved into his home.

After the fall of the empire in 1870, Hugo returned to Paris. There he lived the rest of his life as a literary idol. Huge crowds turned out to celebrate his 80th birthday. Hugo died in Paris on May 22, 1885, and is buried in the Panthéon.

## ALDOUS HUXLEY

(b. 1894—d. 1963)

The English writer and critic Aldous Huxley planned to become a doctor, but an illness that left him partially blind changed those plans. His passion for science served him well in his literary career, however. His novels, poems, essays, and critical works all display a keen interest in the workings of the natural world. He maintained his scientific outlook while also developing mystical beliefs and practices later in his life.

Born on July 26, 1894, in Godalming, Surrey, England, Aldous Leonard Huxley was the grandson of the biologist Thomas H. Huxley, brother of biologist and philosopher Julian, nephew of Mrs. Humphry Ward, and great-nephew of Matthew Arnold. While attending Eton he became partially blind owing to keratitis, but he retained enough eyesight to read with difficulty. He graduated from Balliol College, Oxford, in 1916. He published his first book in 1916 and worked on the periodical *Athenaeum* from 1919 to 1921. Thereafter he devoted himself largely to his own writing and spent much of his time in Italy until the late 1930s, when he settled in California.

In Huxley's pessimistic worldview, society had become callous and harsh. Many of his writings reflect his concern with the minimal potential for any individual in modern society. His brilliantly satirical early novels included *Crome Yellow* (1921) and *Antic Hay* (1923), both of which attack the London literary society of the post–World War I period. *Point Counter Point* (1928) and *Brave New World* (1932) are considered two of Huxley's finest works. *Brave New World* portrays a future society based on psychological conditioning. The vision is horrifying, and the novel is considered one of the best examples of anti-utopian literature. *Eyeless in Gaza* (1936), *Time Must Have a Stop* (1944), and *Brave New World Revisited* (1958) all reflect Huxley's interest in mysticism. His volumes of poetry include *Leda and Other Poems* (1920), *Apennine* (1930), and *The Cicadas and Other Poems* (1931).

Huxley traveled widely and spoke French, Spanish, Italian, and German fluently. In his search for a spiritual center, he experimented with LSD and other drugs and pursued studies of the occult. One of his important later works, *The Doors of Perception* (1954), describes his experiences with the hallucinogenic drug mescaline. He died on November 22, 1963, in Los Angeles, California.

# WASHINGTON IRVING

(b. 1783—d. 1859)

Essayist, historian, and writer of stories, Washington Irving was the first of the great American writers. Before his time Europe had regarded American authors chiefly as curiosities. It was quick to recognize this new writer, however, so graceful was his style and so fascinating and delicate was his humor.

Irving was born on April 3, 1783, in New York, New York, then a town of about 25,000, part of whom were Dutch and part English. It was from this town that he drew much of the material for his stories and sketches. While a boy, he spent many hours rambling about the country regions that he later described. Sometimes he also listened to the folktales told by the Dutch descendants. At home he read a great deal in his father's large library. A great part of his life was a struggle against ill health, grief, and work that he did not like. The day had not yet come when an American author could hope to support himself by his writing alone. There was no copyright law to protect his work.

Irving began the study of law, but in 1804–06 he took an extended tour of Europe. After he returned to the United States, he wrote a humorous group of sketches entitled *Salmagundi*. In 1809 his comic *History of New York from the Beginning of the World to the End of the Dutch Dynasty* appeared. In 1811 Irving moved to Washington, D.C., as a lobbyist for the Irving brothers' hardware-importing firm. During that time he also prepared an American edition of Thomas Campbell's poems and edited the *Analectic Magazine*. In 1815 Irving went to Liverpool, England, on business for his brothers. During his time abroad he met many famous writers and gained new inspiration and encouragement.

Irving subsequently set about writing in earnest. The result was *The Sketch Book of Geoffrey Crayon, Gent* (1819–20), a collection of stories and essays that mix satire and whimsicality with fact and fiction. Although most of the stories revolve around Irving's impressions of England, the collection also contains tales dealing with American subjects. Of these, "The Legend of Sleepy Hollow" and "Rip Van Winkle" have been called the first American short stories. They are both Americanized versions of German folktales, the former a ghost story of a headless horseman and the latter a recounting of a man who falls asleep, only to reawaken 20 years later. The tremendous success of *The Sketch Book* in both England and the United States assured Irving that he could support himself with his writing. In 1822 he produced *Bracebridge Hall*, a sequel to *The Sketch Book*.

In 1826 Irving became involved with the American diplomatic mission in Spain. While there he wrote *Columbus* (1828), followed by *The Companions of Columbus* (1831). Meanwhile, he had become absorbed in the legends of the Moorish past and wrote *A Chronicle of the Conquest of Granada* (1829) and *The Alhambra* (1832), a Spanish counterpart to *The Sketch Book*.

Irving eventually returned to New York in 1832, where he was warmly received. He made a journey west and produced *A Tour of the Prairies* (1835), *Astoria* (1836), and *The Adventures of Captain Bonneville* (1837). Except for the years 1842 to 1846, which he spent as minister to Spain, Irving spent the remainder of his life at his home in Tarrytown, New York, on the Hudson River. There he devoted himself to literary pursuits. He died in Tarrytown on November 28, 1859.

## HENRY JAMES

(b. 1843—d. 1916)

One of the most productive and influential American writers, Henry James was a master of fiction. He enlarged the form, was innovative with it, and placed upon it the mark of a highly individual method and style.

James was born on April 15, 1843, in New York City, the younger brother of American philosopher and psychologist William James. He had two other brothers and one sister. His father, Henry, had inherited wealth, and the family enjoyed a life of leisure. The elder James lectured and wrote, largely about religious matters.

The James children were educated by private teachers, and Henry entered Harvard Law School in 1862. At first Henry seemed to have no definite idea of how he would use his many talents. He was just as interested in drawing and mathematics as he was in writing. At Harvard, however, under the influence of Charles Eliot Norton and William Dean Howells, he decided that literature would be his life's work.

From 1865 to 1869 he wrote criticism and short stories. After much travel, he decided in 1875 to live in Europe. He went first to Paris but in 1876 settled in London. James received an honorary degree from Harvard in 1911 and one from Oxford in 1912. Angry at the United States for not entering World War I at its start, he became a British citizen in 1915.

Because he wrote of a society of sophistication and culture, Henry James was accused of being a snobbish writer. He maintained, however, that it was only this kind of society that had the leisure to indulge in the delicate personal relationships in which he was interested. He wrote of these relationships with great psychological skill and in precise language, usually seeking to involve the reader in the thoughts and outlook of one character.

James wrote 20 novels, 112 shorter works, and 12 plays. The theme of much of his writing was the clash between the innocence and exuberance of the New World with the corruption and wisdom of the Old. His themes also included personal relationships, which he explored in *The Portrait of a Lady*, published in 1881, and social reform, of which he wrote in *The Bostonians* and *The Princess Casamassima* (both 1886). Some of his other works included *Daisy Miller* (1878), *Washington Square* (1880), *The Turn of the Screw* (1898), *The Wings of the Dove* (1902), and *The Ambassadors* (1903). James died on Februart 28, 1916, in London. His ashes were taken to the United States and buried in Cambridge, Massachusetts.

## P.D. JAMES

(b. 1920—d. 2014)

In January 1991, British mystery writer Phyllis Dorothy James White became Baroness James, but her readers recognized the novelist wrapped in the ermine robes of the conservative House of Lords as P.D. James, Britain's acclaimed queen of crime. The matronly grandmother, senior civil servant, and devout Anglican communicant had published her 11th novel, *Devices and Desires*, which manifested her continuing fascination with murder, the sick, and the macabre. James admitted that death had always intrigued her. As a child she had speculated whether Humpty Dumpty had fallen or was pushed.

James was born in Oxford, Oxfordshire, England, on August 3, 1920, the daughter of a tax official. She ended her formal education at Cambridge Girls' High School. Lack of money prevented university study; James worked in a tax office and then as assistant stage manager at the Cambridge Festival Theatre. In 1941 she married Ernest Conner Bantry White and moved to London. Her husband, who died in 1964, served in the Royal Army Medical Corps and returned home with a mental illness from which he never fully recovered. James became the sole support of the family, which included two daughters. In addition to writing, James served as an administrator (1949–68) with the National Health Service and as principal (1968) of the Home Office, working in the Police Department (1968–72) and the Criminal Policy Department (1972–79). James served on the literary advisory committee of the British Arts Council and as a governor of the BBC.

While James always wanted to write, circumstances consistently prevented her from doing so, but as she approached the age of 40, she felt compelled to begin. Her background in police work, complemented by her medical expertise, provided James's inclination to create crime novels, but she also believed that the detective genre demanded painstaking construction, a quality that she prized in fiction. James confined her literary efforts to two hours each morning before leaving for work. In 1959 she began her first mystery, *Cover Her Face*. The manuscript was published by Britain's Faber & Faber in 1962 and by Charles Scribner's Sons, New York, in 1966. James had never received a rejection slip.

James's narrative style, described as taut and absorbing, was noted for its psychological insight and evocation of place and atmosphere. The character Commander Adam Dalgliesh of New Scotland Yard appeared in most of her novels as the cool master detective and published poet.

James's awards include the Crime Writers' Association Award, 1967; Silver Dagger Awards, 1971, 1975, 1986; and a Diamond Dagger Award, 1987. James described herself as a "realistic moralist" with the credo that "detective stories are like 20th-century morality plays . . . the values are basic and unambiguous." Among her works are *An Unsuitable Job for a Woman* (1972), *The Skull Beneath the Skin* (1982), *The Children of Men* (1992; filmed 2006), and *Death Comes to Pemberley* (2011). James died on November 27, 2014, in Oxford.

## JAMES JOYCE

(b. 1882—d. 1941)

The Irish-born author James Joyce was one of the greatest literary innovators of the 20th century. His best-known works contain extraordinary experiments both in language and in writing style.

In these works Joyce developed a technique of writing called "stream of consciousness." Using this technique, he ignored orderly sentence structure and attempted to reproduce in words the rambling processes of the human mind.

James Augustine Aloysius Joyce, one of several children of John Stanislaus Joyce, was born in Dublin, Ireland, on February 2, 1882. He was educated in Dublin at Jesuit schools and graduated from what was then known as Royal University. From boyhood he was fascinated by the sounds of words and by the rhythms of speech and song.

When he was in his early twenties, Joyce left Ireland to live in continental Europe. Although he divorced himself from both his homeland and his church, the major source of his literary inspiration was to be his early life in Dublin and the years he spent in its Jesuit schools.

He lived for a time in Paris, France, and then settled in Trieste, Italy. Later he married Nora Barnacle, of Galway, Ireland. Their son and daughter, George and Lucia, were born in Trieste.

Joyce, who is said to have known 17 modern and ancient languages, at times eked out a living as a language instructor. During World War I he took his family to Switzerland, which was neutral in the war. There his struggle for recognition as a writer was complicated by near-blindness. He underwent a long series of operations and had to wear a patch over one eye, which was damaged.

*Chamber Music*, a book of poems, was Joyce's first published work (1907). It was followed in 1914 by *Dubliners*, a collection of cruelly realistic short stories that deal with life in Joyce's native city. In 1916 Joyce's first full-length book in the stream of consciousness technique, *A Portrait of the Artist as a Young Man*, was published as a novel. It is an autobiographical work, though Joyce named the central figure Stephen Dedalus.

Stephen Dedalus is also a central character in *Ulysses*, an enormous work printed in book form in 1922 in Paris, where Joyce made his postwar home. The book re-creates a single day in Dublin in 1904. The language of *Ulysses* is often as disjointed as the images in a dream. It is full of puns, slang, and metaphors. Portions of the book were considered obscene and *Ulysses* was banned for many years in English-speaking countries. Joyce's last work was *Finnegans Wake*, published in 1939 after parts of it had been serialized as *Work in Progress*. It is written almost in an invented language. His critics complained that Joyce had reached the ultimate in obscurity in the writing of *Finnegans Wake*.

Among other works by Joyce is a book of poems, *Pomes Penyeach* (1927). Part of the first draft of *A Portrait of the Artist as a Young Man* appeared in 1944 as *Stephen Hero*.

Joyce spent his last months in Switzerland, where he went in 1940 to escape the German occupation of France. He died in Zürich, Switzerland, on January 13, 1941.

## FRANZ KAFKA

(b. 1883—d. 1924)

The credit for making Franz Kafka internationally famous as a writer of visionary and imaginative fiction belongs to his friend, novelist Max Brod. In Kafka's will, Brod was asked to burn all unpublished manuscripts and to refrain from republishing those already in print. Brod instead edited the manuscripts and had them published.

Kafka was born into a Jewish middle-class family in Prague, Bohemia (now in the Czech Republic), on July 3, 1883. At the University of Prague he received his doctorate in 1906. After spending a short time as a legal apprentice, he went to work for an insurance company. When the long hours of work prevented him from writing, he took a less demanding job with another insurance business and remained there until forced to retire in 1922 because of ill health. He died in a tuberculosis sanatorium in Kierling, Austria, on June 3, 1924.

Kafka was in many ways a solitary figure, isolated in his own mind from any true community of friendship and alienated from his own Jewish heritage. This inner turmoil, as expressed in his continuously popular writings, promoted Kafka into a symbol of the anxiety and alienation that has pervaded much of 20th-century society.

Only a fraction of his total work was published in his lifetime. This includes sections from *Description of a Struggle* published in German in 1909, a chapter from his novel *Amerika* (1913), and two stories:

*Metamorphosis* (1915) and *In the Penal Colony* (1919). His major novels, *The Trial* and *The Castle*, were published after his death.

## JOHN KEATS

(b. 1795—d. 1821)

"Here lies one whose name was writ in water." This is the epitaph that the poet John Keats prepared for himself. He thought of it in the dark days when he felt death drawing near and despaired of winning fame. During his seven years of writing, he had written some of the greatest poems in the English language.

John Keats was born in London, England, on October 31, 1795. His father was a livery-stable keeper. He did not spend his early years close to nature, as did many poets, but in the city of London. There was, however, born in him an intense love of beauty. "A thing of beauty is a joy forever" is the first line of his *Endymion*. In the "Ode on a Grecian Urn," in which he seems to have caught much of the ancient Greeks' worship of beauty, he declares: "Beauty is truth, truth beauty,—that is all Ye know on earth, and all ye need to know." Unlike his contemporaries Percy Bysshe Shelley and William Wordsworth, Keats had no desire to reform the world or to teach a lesson. He was content if he could make his readers see and hear and feel with their own senses the forms, colors, and sounds that his imagination brought forth.

Keats was apprenticed to a surgeon in his youth and studied surgery faithfully for six years, but his heart was elsewhere. "I find I cannot exist without poetry," he wrote, "—without eternal poetry." In 1816 he became acquainted with Leigh Hunt, and through Hunt with Shelley. The next year, at 22, he gave up his profession and devoted the rest of his short life entirely to the writing of poetry.

In 1818 his first long poem, *Endymion*, appeared. It was harshly attacked by the reviewers of the day, who failed to see that its faults were due to immaturity. Other troubles also crowded upon the young poet. He was in money difficulties, and he was tormented by a hopeless love affair. His health had begun to fail. He rapidly developed tuberculosis. In the autumn of 1820 he went to Italy with his friend Joseph Severn. Keats died in Rome on February 23, 1821.

Keats's chief poems are: *Endymion*; "Lines on the Mermaid Tavern;" "Isabella, or The Pot of Basil;" "On a Summer's Day;" "The Eve of Saint Agnes;" "La Belle Dame sans Merci;" "Ode to a Nightingale;" "Ode to Autumn;" *Lamia*; and *Hyperion*. Among his sonnets are "On First Looking into Chapman's Homer" and "When I Have Fears That I May Cease to Be."

## JACK KEROUAC

(b. 1922—d. 1969)

The writer who coined the name Beat Generation and became its leading spokesman was Jack Kerouac. The beat movement, a social and literary experiment, originated in the bohemian artists' colonies around San Francisco, California, and Greenwich Village in New York City in the late 1950s. Its adherents felt alienated from conventional society and often adopted unconventional styles of life.

Kerouac was born Jean-Louis Kerouac in Lowell, Massachusetts, on March 12, 1922, to French-Canadian parents. He went to school in New York City and afterward served in World War II. After the war he became a wanderer, traveling through the United States and Mexico, unwilling to hold a steady job. His first novel, *The Town and the City*, published in 1950, was fairly well received.

Uncomfortable with conventional writing forms, Kerouac developed an unstructured, flowing, and spontaneous style that first made its appearance in *On the Road* (1957). This book, the bible of the Beat Generation, deals with the frenetic travels around the country of young people who, though poor, were in love with life, love, sex, drugs, jazz, and mysticism and completely rejected the standard values of the time.

The book drew public attention to the existence of a widespread subculture of artists, musicians, poets, and eccentrics that Kerouac had met on his travels. *On the Road* made him the culture hero of the movement. Other Beat Generation writers such as Allen Ginsberg and

Lawrence Ferlinghetti also became prominent, especially as the movement was transformed into the counterculture of the 1960s. Like *On the Road*, all of Kerouac's books, including *The Subterraneans* (1958), *Lonesome Traveler* (1960), and *Desolation Angels* (1965), are autobiographical in nature. Kerouac died in St. Petersburg, Florida, on October 21, 1969.

## STEPHEN KING

(b. 1947—d. )

When American novelist and short-story writer Stephen King published *Carrie* in 1974, the novel became an instant success and helped to establish King's reputation as a master of horror literature. *Carrie* was quickly followed by other horror stories, which were often made into highly successful motion pictures.

Stephen Edwin King was born in Portland, Maine, on September 21, 1947. He began writing at an early age, and his imagination was spurred by listening to tales of horror on the radio, watching them in the movies, or reading them in paperbacks. He attended the University of Maine, graduating in 1970 with a bachelor's degree in English. To support himself as he began his professional writing career, he taught and did other odd jobs.

King's first major success came with *Carrie* (1974; film 1976 and 2013), a story about a young girl who uses her power to move objects by telekinesis in order to wreak revenge on her tormentors. This was the first of many novels in which King blended horror, the macabre, fantasy, and science fiction. Among his works were *'Salem's Lot* (1975; TV miniseries 1979 and 2004), *The Shining* (1977; film 1980; TV miniseries 1997), *The Stand* (1978; TV miniseries 1994), *The Dead Zone* (1979; film 1983; TV series 2002–07), *Firestarter* (1980; film 1984), *Cujo* (1981; film 1983), *The Running Man* (1982; film 1987), *Christine* (1983; film 1983), *Thinner* (1984; film 1996), *It* (1986), *Misery* (1987; film 1990), *The Tommyknockers* (1987; TV miniseries 1993), *The Dark Half* (1989; film 1993), *Needful Things* (1991; film 1993), *Dolores Claiborne* (1993; film 1995), *Dreamcatcher* (2001; film 2003), *Cell* (2006), *Duma Key* (2008), *Under the Dome* (2009; TV series 2013–15 ),

Stephen King in 2007.

*Joyland* (2013), and *Doctor Sleep* (2013), a sequel to *The Shining*. Several of these books appeared under the pseudonym Richard Bachmann. King was also the author of a serial novel, *The Dark Tower*; the first installment, *The Gunslinger*, appeared in 1982; an eighth volume was published in 2012.

In his books King explored terror-producing themes, including vampires, rabid dogs, deranged killers, ghosts, biological warfare, and an evil automobile. In some of his later works (particularly *Dolores Claiborne*) he left the horror genre and provided sharply detailed psychological portraits of his major characters, who are up against challenging circumstances. Although some critics called his work undisciplined and inelegant, King was adept at using realistic detail and forceful plotting to engage and scare the reader.

By the early 21st century, King's books had sold an estimated 350 million copies worldwide. He also wrote short stories collected in such volumes as *Night Shift* (1978) and *Just After Sunset* (2008). Some of his novels were adapted for the screen by well-known directors such as John Carpenter, Brian De Palma, and Stanley Kubrick. In 2000 King published On Writing, a book exploring both his own career and the craft of writing. That same year he released *The Plant* solely as an e-book distributed on the Internet. In 2009 his novella *UR* was made available only to users of the Kindle electronic reading device.

## RUDYARD KIPLING

(b. 1865—d. 1936)

Millions of children have spent happy hours with Rudyard Kipling's *The Jungle Books* and *Just So Stories* about the land and people of India long ago. Kipling was a master storyteller. His songs, which are written in a strong marching rhythm, have the same popular style as his other writing.

Rudyard Kipling knew India well. He was born in Bombay on December 30, 1865, when India was part of the British Empire. Beyond the cities and highways of British India, where the English lived, lay strange primitive country. Rudyard and his younger sister, Alice, had an Indian nurse who told them wonderful tales about the jungle animals. These stories remained in the boy's memory.

When Rudyard was about six, he and his sister were sent to England to be educated. They were left in the unhappy home of a retired naval officer at Southsea, where the boy was often punished by being forbidden to read. Rudyard almost ruined his eyes by reading in secret every book he could lay his hands on. In the story "Baa, Baa, Black Sheep," Kipling later described the six miserable years the two children spent in this "house of desolation."

In 1877 his mother came home from India and remade his world. He and his sister were taken to Devonshire to spend the summer with her. The next year his father came home on leave and took Rudyard to see the great Paris Exhibition, the beginning of Kipling's lifelong love of France. At the end of this holiday the boy was sent to the United Service College at Westward Ho in Devonshire to be educated for the army. Rudyard read constantly—French literature, the English Bible, English poets, and storytellers such as Defoe. In this school also he developed a passionate faith in England and the English people. His years at Devonshire are recorded in *Stalky & Co.*, one of the best novels about schoolboys.

Kipling's father was now principal of the Mayo School of Art at Lahore, in northwest India. When Rudyard was almost 17, he joined his family there. He became a reporter on the one daily newspaper in the Punjab, the *Civil and Military Gazette*. To get material for his newspaper articles he traveled around India for about seven years and came to know the country as few other Englishmen did.

Now Kipling began to write poems and short stories about the British soldier in India that established his reputation as a writer. Such books as *Plain Tales from the Hills*, published in 1888, *Soldiers Three* (1888), and *Barrack-Room Ballads* (1892) emerged. The slim volume of *Departmental Ditties* (1886) he edited, printed, published, and sold himself.

In 1890 his book *The Light That Failed* told of his efforts to make a living as a writer. When his reputation was firmly established, he married an American, Caroline Balestier, and started off with her on a trip around the world. They settled in Vermont, where their first child was born, and where Kipling wrote the tales that were to make up his *Jungle*

*Books* (1894, 1895). Kipling's father visited them and made the famous drawings that were published first, with the stories, in St. Nicholas.

Their family physician had once served with the Gloucester fishing fleet, and he persuaded Kipling to go to Gloucester for the annual memorial service for the men who had been lost or drowned during the year. From this experience came the inspiration for *Captains Courageous* (1897).

After four years in America, the Kiplings decided that their real home was in England. They rented a house in a Sussex village, where in 1897 their only son, John, was born.

The story that is known as *Kim* had been in Kipling's mind for years. Now, stimulated by his father's keen interest, he began to write it. The book was first published in 1901.

Long visits to South Africa, where the Kiplings formed a friendship with Cecil Rhodes, and another trip through North America varied the Sussex life. Early in 1902 they bought a house near the Sussex Downs. All around it was land that had been cultivated since before the Norman Conquest. Thus, stories about Roman times, *Puck of Pook's Hill* (1906) and *Rewards and Fairies* (1910), were begun. Volumes of history cannot give the vital impression that these stories give of England's past. Together they form a chain of "scents and sights and sounds" that reaches to the very heart of England and its history.

In 1907 Kipling was awarded the Nobel Prize in Literature. World War I brought personal tragedy when his son was killed fighting in France with the Irish Guards. More and more he withdrew from the active scene, spending the greater part of the year in his Sussex farmhouse. When he was nearly 70 years old, he began to write his autobiography, *Something of Myself*. This curiously revealing book was published a year after his death.

Kipling died on January 18, 1936, in the same month that brought the death of England's king, George V. The writer was buried in Westminster Abbey among England's honored sons.

# D.H. LAWRENCE

(b. 1885—d. 1930)

In the English literature of the 20th century, few writers have been as original or as controversial as D.H. Lawrence. He was a man almost at war with the conventions, moral constraints, and technology of modern civilization. Much of his life was spent in the search for an ideal community of people in which to live. It was a search that failed in spite of his pilgrimages to such places as Italy, Ceylon (now Sri Lanka), Australia, and New Mexico. His quirks of personality, his wandering way of life, and the desire to explore the depths of human relationships brought originality to his novels and poems.

David Herbert Lawrence was born on September 11, 1885, in the mining village of Eastwood, Nottinghamshire, England. With his mother's help he escaped the fate of becoming a miner, and went instead to Nottingham High School and later to the University College at Nottingham. For several years he taught school, but when his first novel, *The White Peacock*, was published in 1911, he left teaching to concentrate on writing. This novel was followed by *The Trespasser* (1912) and the semiautobiographical *Sons and Lovers* (1913), as well as a volume of short stories, *The Prussian Officer and Other Stories* (1914). These works, well done, but of a rather conventional nature, did not sell well but gave him a good reputation with literary critics.

Lawrence's conflict with the literary world began with the publication of *The Rainbow* (1915), which, with its sequel, *Women in Love* (1921), constitute his best work. These novels, intense psychological probings into human relationships, were condemned as obscene and their publication halted. The same fate met his most famous novel, *Lady Chatterley's Lover*, when it was first issued privately in 1928. The full text was not released to the public until 1959. Some few critics hailed his books as brilliant, others condemned them as neurotic and indecent.

Lawrence seemed naturally restless and was constantly looking for the right place to live. He and his wife, Frieda Richthofen Weekley, lived in Europe prior to World War I, spent the war in England, then traveled to Germany, Sicily, Sardinia, Ceylon, Australia, and eventually, New Mexico. He died of tuberculosis in Vence, France, on March 2, 1930.

His other published works include the novels *The Lost Girl* (1920), *Aaron's Rod* (1922), and *The Plumed Serpent* (1926); travel books, *Sea and Sardinia* (1921) and *Mornings in Mexico* (1927); and *Studies in Classic American Literature* (1923).

## HARPER LEE

(b. 1926—d. 2016 )

American writer Harper Lee was nationally acclaimed for her novel *To Kill a Mockingbird* (1960). The plot of the book was based in part on her attorney father's unsuccessful defense of two African American men convicted of murder. The novel was praised for its sensitive treatment of a child's awakening to racism and prejudice in the American South.

Nelle Harper Lee was born on April 28, 1926, in Monroeville, Alabama. She studied law at the University of Alabama (spending a summer as an exchange student at Oxford University in England) without obtaining a degree. After moving to New York City, she worked as an airline reservation clerk but soon received financial help from friends that allowed her to write full-time. With the help of an editor, she transformed a series of short stories into the novel *To Kill a Mockingbird*.

*To Kill a Mockingbird* takes place in a small Alabama town in the 1930s and is told mostly from the point of view of six-year-old Jean Louise ("Scout") Finch. She is the daughter of Atticus Finch, a white lawyer hired to defend Tom Robinson, a black man accused of raping a white woman. By observing the townspeople's reactions to the trial, Scout becomes aware of the hypocrisy and prejudice that exist in the adult world. *To Kill a Mockingbird* received a Pulitzer Prize in 1961. It became a memorable film in 1962 starring Gregory Peck.

After a few years in New York, Lee divided her time between that city and her hometown of Monroeville. She also wrote a few short essays, including *Romance and High Adventure* (1983), devoted to Alabama history.

In 2007 Lee was awarded the Presidential Medal of Freedom. In early 2015 she announced that she would be releasing a second novel later that year titled *Go Set a Watchman*. Lee wrote the book during the 1950s, and it includes many of the characters from *To Kill a Mockingbird*.

# DORIS MAY LESSING

(b. 1919—d. 2013)

The novels and short stories of British writer Doris Lessing are largely concerned with people involved in the social and political upheavals of the 20th century. The semiautobiographical novel *The Golden Notebook* (1962), in which a woman writer attempts to come to terms with the life of her times through her art, is one of her most complex and her most widely read works. Lessing was awarded the Nobel Prize in Literature in 2007.

Doris May Lessing was born on October 22, 1919, in Kermanshah, Persia (now Iran), where her father was serving as a captain in the British Army. The family moved to a farm in Southern Rhodesia (now Zimbabwe), where she lived from 1924 until she settled in England in 1949. *In Pursuit of the English* (1960) tells of her initial months in England, and *Going Home* (1957) describes her reaction to Rhodesia on a return visit. She reflected further on this subject in African Laughter: *Four Visits to Zimbabwe* (1992). Her early years (through 1949) are chronicled in *Under My Skin* (1994), an autobiography.

Lessing's first published book, *The Grass Is Singing* (1950), is about a white farmer and his wife and their African servant in Rhodesia. Many critics consider her series of novels about Martha Quest—who also grows up in southern Africa and settles in England—her most substantial work. Called Children of Violence, the series comprises *Martha Quest* (1952), *A Proper Marriage* (1954), *A Ripple from the Storm* (1958), *Landlocked* (1965), and *The Four-Gated City* (1969). A master of the short story, Lessing published several collections, including *Five* (1953) and *The Story of a Non-Marrying Man* (1972); *This Was the Old Chief's Country* (1951) and *The Sun Between Their Feet* (1973) contain many of her African stories.

Lessing turned to science fiction in a five-novel sequence titled

Doris Lessing.

*Canopus in Argos: Archives* (1979–83). The novels *The Diary of a Good Neighbour* (1983) and *If the Old Could...* (1984) were published under the pseudonym Jane Somers to dramatize the problems of unknown writers. Her later novels include *The Good Terrorist* (1985), *The Fifth Child* (1988), *Love, Again* (1996), and *Ben, in the World* (2000). *The Sweetest Dream* (2001) is a semiautobiographical novel set primarily in London, England, during the 1960s, while the parable-like novel *The Cleft* (2007) considers the origins of human society. Her collection of essays *Time Bites* (2004) displays her wide-ranging interests, from women's issues and politics to Sufism. *Alfred and Emily* (2008) is a mix of fiction and memoir centered on her parents. Lessing died on November 17, 2013, in London.

# C.S. Lewis

(b. 1898—d. 1963)

The death of C.S. Lewis on Nov. 22, 1963, was not much noticed at the time, because it occurred on the same day as the assassination of United States President John F. Kennedy. Yet for three decades Lewis had been one of the most widely read authors on Christian teaching in the Western world.

Clive Staples Lewis was born in Belfast, Ireland, on November 29, 1898. He was educated by private tutor and then at Malvern College in England for a year before attending University College, Oxford, in 1916. His education was interrupted by service in World War I. In 1918 he returned to Oxford where he did outstanding work as a classical scholar. He taught at Magdalen College, Oxford, from 1925 to 1954, and from 1954 until his death in Oxford he was professor of medieval and Renaissance English at Cambridge University in Cambridge. He was highly respected in his field of study, both as a teacher and writer. His book *The Allegory of Love: a Study in Medieval Tradition*, published in 1936, is considered by many to be his best work.

It was as an apologist for Christianity that Lewis gained his greatest audience. In his attempt to formulate a core of Christian understanding, Lewis wrote a number of highly readable books—intelligent, imaginative, and often witty. Among these were: *The Pilgrim's Regress*, published in 1933; *The Problem of Pain* (1940); *Miracles* (1947); and *The Screwtape Letters* (1942), probably his most popular work. He also wrote a trilogy of religious science fiction novels: *Out of the Silent Planet* (1938), *Perelandra* (1943), and *That Hideous Strength* (1945). For children he wrote a series of seven allegorical tales, (*The Chronicles of Narnia*) beginning with *The Lion, the Witch, and the Wardrobe* in 1950. His autobiography, *Surprised by Joy*, was published in 1955.

# JACK LONDON

(b. 1876—d. 1916)

The novelist and short-story writer Jack London was, in his lifetime, one of the most popular authors in the world. After World War I his fame was eclipsed in the United States by a new generation of writers, but he remained popular in many other countries, especially in the Soviet Union, for his romantic tales of adventure mixed with elemental struggles for survival.

John Griffith London was born in San Francisco on January 12, 1876. His family was poor, and he was forced to go to work early in life to support himself. At 17 he sailed to Japan and Siberia on a seal-hunting voyage. He was largely self-taught, reading voluminously in libraries and spending a year at the University of California. In the late 1890s he joined the gold rush to the Klondike. This experience gave him material for his first book, *The Son of Wolf*, published in 1900, and for *Call of the Wild* (1903), one of his most popular stories.

In his writing career of 17 years, London produced 50 books and many short stories. He wrote mostly for money, to meet ever-increasing expenses. His fame as a writer gave him a ready audience as a spokesman for a peculiar and inconsistent blend of socialism and racial superiority.

London's works, all hastily written, are of uneven quality. The best books are the Klondike tales, which also include *White Fang* (1906) and *Burning Daylight* (1910). His most enduring novel is probably the autobiographical *Martin Eden* (1909), but the exciting *Sea Wolf* (1904) continues to have great appeal for young readers.

In 1910 London settled near Glen Ellen, California, where he intended to build his dream home, "Wolf House." After the house burned down before completion in 1913, he was a broken and sick man. He died on November 22, 1916, in Glen Ellen. The official cause of death was listed as uremia.

# NICCOLÒ MACHIAVELLI

(b. 1469—d. 1527)

The term "Machiavellian" refers to someone who is unscrupulous, cunning, cynical, and unprincipled. The adjective would have dismayed Niccolò Machiavelli, from whose name it is derived. He was one of the brightest lights of the Italian Renaissance, a writer of powerful, influential, and thoughtful prose who was devoted to truth and to the freedom of Florence, the city he loved. He has been so misunderstood because the motives and language of his chief works—*The Prince* and *Discourses on Livy*, both published in 1513—have been seriously misinterpreted. Machiavelli had a tragic sense of human wickedness and despaired of seeing virtue triumph. This pessimism often led him to express himself more bluntly than he might otherwise have done. He was, above all, a realist when it came to understanding human nature. His reflections on mankind and its past made him a founder of the philosophy of history.

Machiavelli was born in Florence on May 3, 1469. Because of his family's poverty he received most of his education at home. In 1498 he was given a government position in the city and remained in its service for 13 years.

Frequently he was used as a roving ambassador, trying to protect the interests of Florence from being sacrificed to the warring parties of Europe: France, the Holy Roman Empire, and the Roman Catholic church. One of his most vital contributions to the welfare of Florence was persuading the city to raise its own militia instead of using a mercenary, or hired, army. He was vindicated when his militia helped conquer Pisa in 1509.

When Giuliano de' Medici became ruler of Florence in 1512, Machiavelli lost his post. He went to live on his property outside the city and spent the time writing his two masterpieces as well as a comedy, *The Mandrake* (1518). Cardinal Giulio de' Medici, later Pope Clement VII, came to govern Florence in 1520, and the writer was restored to government service. In honor of his patron, Lorenzo Strozzi, he wrote *On the Art of War* (1521), a treatise that laid the foundations of modern military tactics. When the Medici were cast off in 1527, Machiavelli was again turned out of office because he had served a Medici. He died on June 21, 1527.

## THOMAS MANN

(b. 1875—d. 1955)

A great German novelist, Thomas Mann was as well known abroad as he was in Germany. During his lifetime his works were translated into many languages. His books were particularly popular in the United States.

Thomas Mann was born on June 6, 1875, in Lübeck, Germany. His father was a prosperous grain merchant. His mother, a talented musician, was born in Brazil. He was one of five children. He and his older brother, Heinrich, both began writing at an early age. Heinrich also became a well-known writer. When Thomas was 15 his father died and his mother moved to Munich.

At age 25 Thomas Mann had a great success with his first full-length novel, *Buddenbrooks*. The story depicts the social decline through three generations of an upper-class Lübeck family similar to his own. His *Death in Venice* was published in 1912. This symbolic novel traces the decline of an infatuated and aging writer against the background of a beautiful but plague-stricken city.

In 1905 Mann married Katja Pringsheim, the daughter of a Munich University professor. They had six children. His wife's experiences in a tuberculosis sanitarium in the Alps gave Mann material for his novel *The Magic Mountain*, published in 1924. In this philosophical novel the patients, of various nationalities, have brilliant discussions and profound emotional experiences. They make up a miniature Europe of clashing ideas and decaying culture. In 1929 Mann was awarded the Nobel Prize in Literature.

Mann and his wife were away from Germany on a vacation in 1933 when Adolf Hitler came to power. Erika, their oldest daughter, warned them by telephone not to return. The Nazis condemned Mann's works as un-German. They confiscated his house and deprived him of his citizenship. The children escaped, and the family lived in France and Switzerland until 1938. That year Princeton University appointed Mann a lecturer in the humanities, and the family moved to the United States. They settled in California in 1941. In 1944 Mann became a citizen of the United States. Throughout World War II he strongly attacked the Nazi system. After the war, Mann visited both East and West Germany and received many public honors.

In his home in Santa Monica overlooking the Pacific Ocean, Mann completed *Joseph the Provider*, the concluding volume of his monumental *Joseph and His Brothers*. To this four-part novel, based on the brief account in the Bible, Mann brought a wealth of detail derived from modern anthropology, archaeology, and psychoanalysis. He thought it his best work.

After 15 years in the United States, the Manns returned to Europe. Mann died in his home above Lake Zürich in Switzerland on August 12, 1955.

# HERMAN MELVILLE

(b. 1819—d. 1891)

During his four years as a sailor and beachcomber in the South Pacific, Herman Melville gathered rich material for several novels. One of them was *Moby Dick*, the story of Captain Ahab's vengeful search for the white whale that had maimed him. On the surface *Moby Dick* can be read as an exciting adventure story. At a deeper level it is a profound study of humankind's struggle against the forces of evil. Melville developed a complex, highly individual writing style using richly symbolic language. Largely neglected during his lifetime, he is now regarded as one of the greatest of American writers. Melville was an important contributor to the American Renaissance, an outpouring of literary works in the United States in the mid-1800s that helped form the basis of the young country's literature.

Herman Melville was born in New York City, New York, on August

1, 1819, the third of eight children. When the boy was 12, his father died. Herman was silent and slow. His mother considered him a dull child. He finished school when he was 15 and for two years worked at a series of jobs. Then he signed on as cabin boy aboard the ship *St. Lawrence*, bound for Liverpool, England. He left the *St. Lawrence* when it returned to New York, but he could not forget the sea.

In 1841 Melville took a berth as ordinary seaman aboard the whaler *Acushnet*. The ship left Fairhaven, near New Bedford, Massachusetts, for a long voyage around Cape Horn and into the South Pacific. Melville discovered that the seafaring life was harsh and oppressive, and after 18 months Melville and a companion jumped ship at the Marquesas Islands.

For several weeks they lived with the natives and then went aboard an Australian whaler. At Tahiti Melville went ashore, and for about a year he worked as a laborer. Finally he signed on as a seaman on the frigate *United States* and was discharged 14 months later when the ship docked at Boston, Massachusetts.

Almost at once, Melville began to set down his experiences in writing. His adventures in Polynesia were the basis of his successful first novels, *Typee* (1846) and *Omoo* (1847). After his allegorical fantasy *Mardi* (1849) failed, he quickly wrote the novels *Redburn* (1849) and *White-Jacket* (1850), about the rough life of sailors. Unlike his first novels, these last two works had passages of profoundly questioning melancholy. Melville had been reading the plays of Shakespeare, particularly noting somber passages. This reading counterbalanced in him the doctrines of Ralph Waldo Emerson, a Transcendentalist philosopher and writer. Melville had heard lectures on Emerson's general optimism about human goodness. Another important influence was Nathaniel Hawthorne's *The Scarlet Letter*, a novel exploring good and evil in the human being, which Melville read in 1850.

Meanwhile, Melville had married. In 1850 he moved his family from New York to a farm near Pittsfield, Massachusetts. Hawthorne lived nearby, and the two authors became friends. Here Melville wrote *Moby Dick*, his masterpiece.

Melville threw himself into the work and at the end was near collapse from mental exhaustion. *Moby Dick* was published in 1851. This novel is an intense whaling story that features a convincingly imagined tragic hero. Melville's deeper concerns in the novel are the uncertain defeats and triumphs of the human spirit and its combination of creative and murderous urges. The novel can also be read as a symbolic examination of the problems and possibilities of American democracy.

After finishing *Moby Dick*, Melville at once began the novel *Pierre*, published in 1852. It is an intensely personal work about an artist alienated from society. Melville's first, more conventional books were popular, but *Moby Dick* and *Pierre* were attacked by literary critics and virtually ignored by the public.

Melville's income from writing and farming was not enough to support his family, so he tried lecturing. His failure made him draw even closer into himself. At length he became a customs inspector in New York City. He held the post for 19 years. He wrote several volumes of poetry and a number of short stories. Among the finest of these stories are "Benito Cereno" and "Bartleby the Scrivener," which were both included in the collection *The Piazza Tales* (1856). These works reflected Melville's increasing despair and contempt for human hypocrisy and materialism. He completed a powerful, almost morbid short novel, *Billy Budd, Foretopman*, a few months before his death in New York City on September 28, 1891, but the novel was not published until 1924. It tells the story of a sailor, Billy Budd, who is falsely accused of trying to start a mutiny. Billy is hanged but goes willingly to his fate. Evil has not wholly triumphed, however, and Billy's memory lives on as an emblem of good.

For decades Melville's books lay in obscurity. But after World War I students of American literature rediscovered Melville. Today his works enjoy a wide critical and popular audience.

## ARTHUR MILLER

(b. 1915—d. 2005)

One of the most important U.S. playwrights since Eugene O'Neill, Arthur Miller was noted for dramas that combined social awareness with a searching concern for his characters' inner lives. His best-known play, *Death of a Salesman*, debuted in 1949 and was awarded the

Pulitzer Prize for Drama that year.

Miller was born on October 17, 1915, in New York City. After graduation from high school, he worked in a warehouse, and with the money he earned, he attended the University of Michigan at Ann Arbor. His first important play was *All My Sons* (1947), a drama about a manufacturer of faulty war materials. *Death of a Salesman*, the tragedy of an ordinary man destroyed by false values, became one of the most famous American plays of its period.

In 1953 Miller received a Tony Award for *The Crucible*, a play based on the witchcraft trials in Salem, Massachusetts, in 1692. Miller considered that period relevant to the 1950s, when investigation of subversive activities was widespread. Miller himself was called before the House Un-American Activities Committee in 1956, but he refused to name people he had seen at an alleged Communist writers' meeting 10 years earlier. His contempt conviction was later overturned.

Miller staged two short plays, *A Memory of Two Mondays* and *A View from the Bridge*, in 1955. The following year he attracted widespread publicity with his marriage to actress Marilyn Monroe. He wrote the screenplay for what turned out to be Monroe's last film, *The Misfits* (1961). Miller's play *After the Fall* (1964), which features a Monroe-like character, is concerned with failure in human relationships and its consequences.

Among Miller's later plays were *The Price* (1968), *The Creation of the World and Other Business* (1972), *The Archbishop's Ceiling* (1977), *The Ride Down Mt. Morgan* (1991), *Broken Glass* (1994), and *Resurrection Blues* (2002). His final play, again featuring a character based on Monroe, was *Finishing the Picture* (2004). Miller was also the author of a short-story collection, *I Don't Need You Any More* (1967); an autobiography, *Timebends: A Life* (1987); and two essay collections, *The Theater Essays* (1978) and *Echoes Down the Corridor* (2000). He died on February 10, 2005, in Roxbury, Connecticut.

# JOHN MILTON

(b. 1608—d. 1674)

Next to William Shakespeare, John Milton is usually regarded as the greatest English poet.

Milton attended the University of Cambridge (1625–32), where he wrote poems in Latin, Italian, and English; these include the companion poems "L'Allegro" and "Il Penseroso," both written c. 1631. In 1632–39 he engaged in private study—writing the masque *Comus* (first performed 1634) and the elegy "Lycidas" (1638)—and toured Europe, spending most of his time in Italy. Concerned with the republican cause in England, he spent much of 1641–60 pamphleteering for civil and religious liberty and serving in Oliver Cromwell's government. Milton's best-known prose is in the pamphlets *Areopagitica*, on freedom of the press, and *Of Education* (both 1644). He also wrote tracts on divorce and against the monarchy and the Church of England. He lost his sight c. 1651 and thereafter dictated his works.

John Milton, detail of an engraving by William Faithorne, 1670.

After the Restoration he was arrested as a prominent defender of the Commonwealth but was soon released. *Paradise Lost* (1667, 1674), considered the greatest epic poem in English, uses blank verse and reworks Classical epic conventions to recount the Fall of Man; Milton's characterization of Satan has been widely admired. *Paradise Regained* (1671) is a shorter epic in which Christ overcomes Satan the tempter, and *Samson Agonistes* (1671) is a dramatic poem in which the Old Testament figure conquers self-pity and despair to become God's champion. *History of Britain* was incomplete when published in 1670, and an unfinished work on theology was discovered in 1823. The exact date and location of Milton's death remains unknown.

## TONI MORRISON

(b. 1931—d. )

U.S. author Toni Morrison was noted for her examination of the African American experience (particularly the female experience) within the black community. Her use of fantasy, her intricate poetic style, and her rich interweaving of the mythic gave her stories great strength and texture. In 1993 she won the Nobel Prize in Literature.

Morrison was born Chloe Anthony Wofford on February 18, 1931, in Lorain, Ohio. She grew up in a poor family but graduated from Howard University in Washington, D.C., in 1953 and received a master's degree in English from Cornell University in Ithaca, New York, in 1955. After several years as an English instructor, Morrison became an editor and wrote in her spare time.

Morrison's first novel, *The Bluest Eye* (1970), was a criticism of middle-class black life and of human intolerance. With the 1977 publication of *Song of Solomon*, which is told by a male narrator in search of his identity, Morrison received popular as well as critical acclaim. *Tar Baby* (1981), set on a Caribbean island, explores conflicts of race, class, and sex. *Beloved* won the 1988 Pulitzer Prize for Fiction. It is based on the true story of a runaway slave who, at the point of recapture, kills her infant daughter in order to spare her a life of slavery. Morrison's later works include *A Mercy* (2008), which deals with slavery in 17th-century America, and *Home* (2012), about a traumatized Korean War veteran who encounters racism after returning home and later overcomes apathy to rescue his sister.

Toni Morrison, 2014.

Besides her novels, Morrison published a work of criticism, *Playing in the Dark: Whiteness and the Literary Imagination*, in 1992. Many of her essays and speeches were collected in *What Moves at the Margin: Selected Nonfiction* (edited by Carolyn C. Denard), published in 2008. In addition, Morrison released several children's books, including *Who's Got Game?: The Ant or the Grasshopper?* and *Who's Got Game?: The Lion or the Mouse?*, both written with her son and published in 2003. *Remember* (2004), also aimed at children, uses archival photographs to chronicle the hardships of black students during the integration of the U.S. public school system. Morrison also wrote the libretto for *Margaret Garner* (2005), an opera about the same story that inspired *Beloved*.

In 2010 Morrison was made an officer of the French Legion of Honour. Two years later she was awarded the U.S. Presidential Medal of Freedom.

# HARUKI MURAKAMI

(b. 1949—d. )

Japanese novelist and short-story writer Haruki Murakami is known for his eccentric and whimsical writing style. American popular culture, film, and the pulp detective novel genre all have been influences on Murakami's work. His novels and stories often feature bizarre plots and subplots.

Murakami was born in Kyoto, Japan, on January 12, 1949, and grew up in Kobe, Japan. Although he studied Greek drama at Waseda University in Tokyo, Japan, Murakami was strongly attracted to the hardboiled detective fiction of American writers such as Raymond Chandler. Murakami graduated in 1975. Rejecting a life in which he would spend long hours in an office as a "salaryman," he opened a jazz café. In the evenings he wrote.

Murakami's first novel, *Kaze no uta o kike* (*Hear the Wind Sing*), was published in 1979. It won a prize for best fiction by a new writer and was filmed in 1980. His first internationally acclaimed novel, *Hitsuji o meguru boken* (*A Wild Sheep Chase*), was published in 1982. The book is part mystery, part comedy, and part fantasy. It acquires an eerie quality from the mysterious sheep that comes to possess the narrator's friend, known as "the Rat." The narrator and the Rat reappear in Murakami's next important novel, *Sekai no owari to hadoboirudo wandarando* (1985; *Hard-Boiled Wonderland and the End of the World.*). This fantasy novel was both popular and critically acclaimed, winning the celebrated Tanizaki Prize.

By the 1980s, Murakami had developed a loyal following in Japan, the United States, and elsewhere. His works were translated into Chinese, Korean, English, and other languages. His coming-of-age novel *Noruwei no mori* (1987; *Norwegian Wood*) sold millions of copies in Japan and firmly established him as a literary celebrity. It was filmed in 2010.

In 1991 Murakami left Japan to take a teaching position in the United States. While teaching at Princeton University (1991–93) and Tufts University (1993–95), he wrote one of his most ambitious novels, *Nejimaki-dori kuronikuru* (*The Wind-Up Bird Chronicle*). It was published in 1994–95. This story represents a departure from his usual themes. It is devoted in part to depicting Japanese military aggression in Asia during World War II as a nightmare.

In 1995 Murakami moved back to Japan. He was prompted to return by a destructive earthquake in Kobe and a poison-gas attack carried out by the AUM Shinrikyo religious sect on a Tokyo subway. In 1997 Murakami wrote his first nonfiction work, *Andaguraundo* (*Underground*), a series of interviews with victims of the AUM Shinrikyo terrorist attack. His book *Kami no kodomo-tachi wa mina odoru* (2000; *After the Quake*) is a collection of six short stories exploring the psychological effects of the Kobe earthquake on residents of Japan.

In 1999 Murakami published *Suputoniku no koibito* (*Sputnik Sweetheart*), a bleak tale about a love triangle. His later novels include *Umibe no Kafuka* (2002; *Kafka on the Shore*) and *Afuta daku* (2004; *After Dark*). His novel *1Q84* (2009) shifts between two characters as they navigate an alternate reality of their own making. The book's themes range from the September 11 attacks to vigilante justice. Its title is a reference to George Orwell's novel *Nineteen Eighty-four* (1949).

Murakami's short stories have been translated into English in the collections *The Elephant Vanishes* (1993) and *Blind Willow, Sleeping Woman* (2006). In 2007 he published a memoir, *Hashiru koto ni tsuite kataru toki ni boku no kataru koto* (*What I Talk About When I Talk About Running*), that centers on his love for marathon running. An experienced translator of American literature, Murakami also published editions in Japanese of works by Raymond Carver, Paul Theroux, Truman Capote, Ursula K. Le Guin, and J.D. Salinger.

## VLADIMIR NABOKOV

(b. 1899—d. 1977)

The Russian-born American writer Vladimir Nabokov would probably have remained a fairly obscure novelist had it not been for his authorship of *Lolita*, published in 1955. Because of the furor this novel raised with critics and public alike, it became widely read, and it was eventually made into a play and a motion picture. The seemingly scandalous story line is simple: the antihero Humbert Humbert's passion for young girls. But the novel is in no way pornographic. It is a parody: true love is examined in the light of its opposite. The whole body of Nabokov's writings has been characterized as dealing with problems of art masked by allegory. The plots are devices by which he examined the nature of art itself.

Vladimir Vladimirovich Nabokov was born in Russia on April 23, 1899. His father was a prerevolutionary liberal politician and author. Young Nabokov grew up in St. Petersburg. His father opposed the Bolshevik government that came to power in 1917, and the family moved to Berlin, Germany, in 1919. The family went on to England, where Nabokov entered Cambridge University. He graduated in 1922, the same year his father was killed by a political assassin in Berlin. Nabokov rejoined his family and lived in Germany and France until 1940, when World War II was under way. He had published collections of poetry in the early 1920s. His first novel, *Mashenka (Mary)*, came out in 1926. It was followed by *King, Queen, Knave* (1928) and *The Defense* (1930). In 1925 he married Véra Slonim, a translator. Their son, Dmitri, was an opera singer and sports car racer and translated many of his father's works.

In 1940 Nabokov moved to the United States, where he taught literature. Most of his early work was written in Russian, but he also wrote novels in English—*The Real Life of Sebastian Knight* (1941), *Bend Sinister* (1947), *Pnin* (1957), *Pale Fire* (1962), *Ada* (1969), *Glory* (1971), and *Transparent Things* (1972)—as well as novellas and short stories. In 1945 Nabokov became a United States citizen. *Conclusive Evidence* (1951; revised as *Speak, Memory*, 1966) is an account of his early life. He died on July 2, 1977, in Montreux, Switzerland, where he lived from 1961.

## V.S. NAIPAUL

(b. 1932—d. )

The novels of V.S. Naipaul are about individuals in developing countries who are seeking an identity and trying to make sense of their lives. His nonfiction works follow a similar theme, dealing with postcolonial societies that are in conflict, searching for a future that is altogether uncertain—and often sinking into violence and repression. Throughout his works, one finds an unflinching portrayal of the problems wrought by imperialism and the shattering effect these have on everyday people. Naipaul was knighted by Queen Elizabeth in 1990 and was awarded the Nobel Prize in Literature in 2001.

Vidiadhar Surajprasad Naipaul was born in Caguanas, Trinidad, on August 17, 1932. He attended school in Port of Spain and then went to England in 1950 to study at Oxford University. After graduation he settled in London, where he worked at a variety of jobs before gaining success as a writer. His first work, *The Mystic Masseur*, was published in 1957 and established his gift for portraying street life. His next efforts, such as *The Suffrage of Elvira* (1958) and *Miguel Street* (1959), were similar in their ironic accounts of life in the Caribbean region.

In his next novel, *A House for Mr. Biswas* (1961), he used his father's experiences in Trinidad to portray a Brahmin Indian living halfway around the world from home. Naipaul won Britain's Booker Prize for *In a Free State* (1971), a book of three stories set in different countries. Subsequent novels include *A Bend in the River* (1979), *Finding the Center* (1984), and *The Enigma of Arrival* (1987). The latter work, considered by some to be his masterpiece, is somewhat autobiographical in its portrayal of a writer from the Caribbean who travels to the countryside of England. Later fiction included *A Way in the World* (1994) and *Half a Life* (2001), a novel about an Indian immigrant to England and then Africa. This immigrant becomes "half a person," as Naipaul has said, "living a borrowed life." Naipaul published *Magic Seeds*, a sequel to *Half a Life*, in 2004.

In his nonfiction works, Naipaul used a literary style to draw his readers into the world of his subjects. Among his nonfiction works are *The Return of Eva Perón* (1980), *Among the Believers: An Islamic Journey* (1981), *India: A Million Mutinies Now* (1991), *Beyond Belief: Islamic Excursions Among the Converted Peoples* (1998), *Reading and Writing: A Personal Account* (2000), *The Writer and the World* (2002), *Literary Occasions* (2003), and *The Masque of Africa* (2010).

# JOYCE CAROL OATES

(b. 1938—d. )

Prolific American novelist, short-story writer, and essayist, Joyce Carol Oates was noted for writing in a variety of styles and genres. Her depictions of violence and evil in modern society were particularly effective.

Oates was born on June 16, 1938, in Lockport, New York. In college she studied English, receiving a bachelor's degree in 1960 from Syracuse University and a master's degree the next year from the University of Wisconsin. Oates taught English at the University of Detroit from 1961 to 1967 and at the University of Windsor in Ontario, Canada, from 1967 to 1978. From 1978 she taught at Princeton University in New Jersey. In 1961 she married Raymond J. Smith (died 2008), a fellow English student who became a professor and an editor. With him she publishedthe *Ontario Review*, a literary magazine.

Early in her career Oates contributed short stories to a number of magazines and reviews, including the *Prairie Schooner* and *Literary Review*. In 1963 she published her first collection of short stories, *By the North Gate*. Her first novel, *With Shuddering Fall*, appeared in 1964 and was followed by a second short-story collection, *Upon the Sweeping Flood* (1965). She wrote constantly thereafter, averaging about two books per year. Her fiction works include *them* (1969; winner of a National Book Award), *Do with Me What You Will* (1973), *Black Water* (1992), *We Were the Mulvaneys* (1996), *Broke Heart Blues* (1999), *The Falls* (2004), *My Sister, My Love: The Intimate Story of Skyler Rampike* (2008), *Mudwoman* (2012), and *Carthage* (2014).

Oates's later short-story collections included *Faithless: Tales of Transgression* (2001) and *High Lonesome: New & Selected Stories, 1966–2006* (2006). *Wild Nights!: Stories About the Last Days of Poe, Dickinson, Twain, James, and Hemingway* (2008) featured fictionalized accounts of the final days of various American writers. The stories in *Black Dahlia and White Rose* (2012) were threaded with menace and violence.

Oates also wrote mysteries (under the pseudonyms Rosamond Smith

Joyce Carol Oates.

and Lauren Kelly), plays, essays, poetry, and literary criticism. Essays, reviews, and other prose pieces are included in *Where I've Been, and Where I'm Going* (1999) and in *In Rough Country* (2010). In 2011 Oates published the memoir *A Widow's Story,* in which she mourned her husband's death. Her work for young adults included *Big Mouth & Ugly Girl* (2002) and *Two or Three Things I Forgot to Tell You* (2012).

# FLANNERY O'CONNOR

(b. 1925—d. 1964)

American novelist and short-story writer Flannery O'Connor usually set her works in the rural American South and often wrote about the relationship between the individual and God. Her fiction, misunderstood by many at first because of its religious themes and frequent violence, came to be widely read.

Mary Flannery O'Connor was born on March 25, 1925, in Savannah, Georgia, and grew up in a prominent Roman Catholic family. She lived in Savannah until her adolescence, but the worsening of her father's lupus erythematosus forced the family to relocate in 1938 to the home in rural Milledgeville, Georgia, where her mother had been raised. After graduating from Georgia State College for Women (now Georgia College & State University) in 1945, O'Connor studied creative writing at the University of Iowa Writers' Workshop.

O'Connor's first published work, a short story, appeared in the magazine *Accent* in 1946. Her first novel was *Wise Blood* (1952; film 1979). It consists of a series of near-independent chapters, many of which originated in previously published short stories. The story follows a man who returns home from military service and founds the Church Without Christ, which leads to a series of interactions with the grotesque inhabitants of his hometown. With the publication of further short stories, first collected in *A Good Man Is Hard to Find, and Other Stories* (1955), O'Connor came to be regarded as a master of the form. The short story "A Good Man Is Hard to Find" has become possibly her best-known work. In it O'Connor creates an unexpected agent of salvation in the character of an escaped convict called The Misfit, who kills a quarreling family on vacation in the Deep South. O'Connor's other works of fiction included a novel, *The Violent Bear It Away* (1960), and the short-story collection *Everything That Rises Must Converge* (1965).

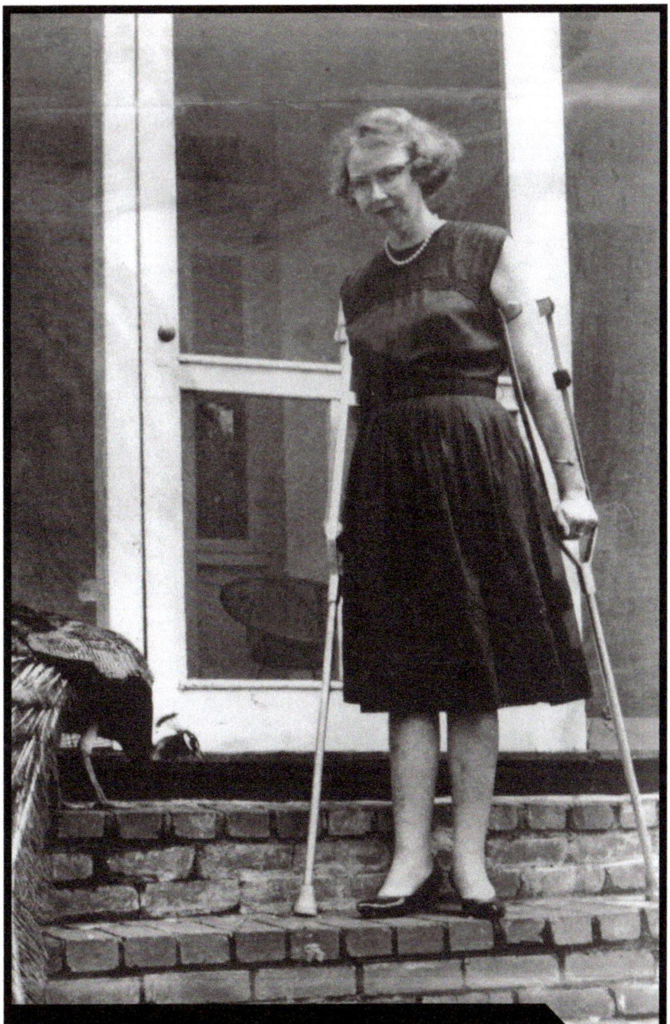

Flannery O'Connor.

O'Connor died on August 3, 1964, in Milledgeville from the lupus erythematosus that she inherited from her father. Several volumes collecting her work were published posthumously. A collection of occasional prose pieces, *Mystery and Manners,* appeared in 1969. *The Complete Stories* (1971) contained several stories that had not previously appeared in book form; it won a National Book Award in 1972. *The Habit of Being* (1979) was a book of her letters, *The Presence of Grace, and Other Book Reviews* (1983) contained her book reviews and correspondence with local diocesan newspapers, and *A Prayer Journal* (2013) collected private religious meditations.

# GEORGE ORWELL

(b. 1903—d. 1950)

As a journalist and writer of autobiographical narratives, George Orwell was outstanding. But he will be remembered primarily for two works of fiction that have become 20th-century classics: *Animal Farm*, published in 1944, and *Nineteen Eighty-four* (1949).

George Orwell is a pen name. His real name was Eric Arthur Blair, and he was born in 1903 at Montihari in Bengal, India, where his father was a minor British official. His family had social status but little money, a fact that influenced Orwell's later attitude toward the English class system and the empire's treatment of its subject peoples. In about 1911 the family returned to England. Blair was sent to school in Sussex, where he was distinguished both by his poverty and his intelligence. He later wrote of his miserable school years in *Such, Such Were the Joys* (1953). He attended Eton in the years 1917 to 1921 but decided against going on to a university. Instead he went to Burma (now Myanmar) as a member of the British imperial police.

His own poverty, plus his growing aversion to Britain's imperial policies, led him to resign from the government in 1928. He then spent several years among the poor and outcast of Europe and among the unemployed miners in the north of England. These experiences were recounted in *Down and Out in Paris and London* (1933) and *The Road to Wigan Pier* (1937). Then Orwell went to Spain to report on the Spanish Civil War. His experiences in Spain were described in *Homage to Catalonia* (1938), one of his best books.

During World War II Orwell wrote for the British Broadcasting Company and worked as a literary editor for the London *Tribune*. The success of *Animal Farm* in 1944 allowed him to devote himself to writing. He bought a house on the island of Jura, where he wrote *Nineteen Eighty-four*. By the time it was published, Orwell was already ill from the tuberculosis from which he died on January 21, 1950, in London.

# SYLVIA PLATH

(b. 1932—d. 1963)

U.S. poet and novelist Sylvia Plath's best-known poems are carefully crafted pieces noted for their personal imagery and intense focus. Many concern such themes as alienation, death, and self-destruction. She was little known at the time of her death by suicide, but by the mid-1970s she was considered a major contemporary poet.

Plath was born on October 27, 1932, in Boston, Massachusetts, to Aurelia Schober, a teacher, and Otto Emil Plath, a professor of entomology. Otto Plath died in 1940 after a long illness, and his death was a negative formative factor in Plath's life. Plath published her first poem in the *Boston Traveller* at age 8. She entered and won many literary contests and while still in high school sold her first short story, to *Seventeen* magazine.

She entered Smith College on a scholarship in 1951 and was a cowinner of the *Mademoiselle* magazine fiction contest in 1952. Despite her remarkable artistic, academic, and social success at Smith, Plath suffered from severe depression and attempted suicide by taking an overdose of sleeping pills. She survived the attempt and was admitted to a mental hospital for severe depression. She graduated from Smith with highest honors in June 1955 and went on to Newnham College, Cambridge, in England, on a Fulbright fellowship. In 1956 she married the English poet Ted Hughes. For the following two years she was an instructor in English at Smith College. In 1960, shortly after Plath and her husband returned to England, her first collection of poems appeared as *The Colossus*. Her second book, a strongly autobiographical novel titled *The Bell Jar*, was published in 1963 under the pseudonym "Victoria Lucas." The book describes the mental breakdown, attempted suicide, and eventual recovery of a young college girl.

During her last three years Plath abandoned the restraints and conventions that had bound much of her early work. She wrote with great speed, producing poems of stark self-revelation and confession. The anxiety, confusion, and doubt that haunted her were transmuted into verses of great power and pathos borne on flashes of incisive wit. Suddenly in 1963, after a burst of productivity, Plath took her own life. (She died on February 11, 1963, in London, England.) *Ariel* (1965), a collection of her later poems, helped spark the growth of something of a cult devoted to Plath. The reissue of *The Bell Jar* under her own name in 1966 and the appearance of small collections of previously unpublished poems, including *Crossing the Water* (1971) and *Winter Trees* (1971), were welcomed by critics and the public alike. *Johnny Panic and the Bible of Dreams*, a book of short stories and prose, was published in 1977, and *The Collected Poems*, which includes many previously unpublished poems, appeared in 1981. *The It-Doesn't-Matter Suit*, a book for children, was also discovered among her papers and published posthumously. In 1998 Hughes published a collection of poems exploring his relationship with Plath, entitled *Birthday Letters*.

## EDGAR ALLAN POE

(b. 1809—d. 1849)

The greatest American teller of mystery and suspense tales in the 19th century was Edgar Allan Poe. In his mysteries he invented the modern detective story. In Poe's poems, like his tales, his characters are tortured by nameless fears and longings. Today Poe is acclaimed as one of America's greatest writers, but in his own unhappy lifetime he knew little but failure.

Edgar Poe was born in Boston, Massachusetts, on January 19, 1809. His parents were touring actors. Orphaned at age three, he was taken into the home of John Allan, a merchant of Richmond, Virginia. His wife reared Edgar as her son, but Allan accepted the boy largely to please her. Later Poe took Allan as his middle name, but his signature was usually Edgar A. Poe.

John Allan became one of the richest men in Virginia. He never formally adopted Poe, but the youth thought that he would be named Allan's heir. After a time, however, Allan grew cold toward him, and Poe realized that his place in the family was insecure.

Edgar Allan Poe.

When he was 17 Poe entered the University of Virginia. Allan gave Poe only a small allowance, and the young man soon began owing money. He gambled and ran into greater debt. By the end of the year he owed $2,500. He was nervous and unstable, and he began to drink. His body could not tolerate alcohol, and only a small amount made him at first intoxicated and later ill. Allan angrily withdrew Poe from school, and a few months later Poe left home.

Poe went to Boston in 1827. He persuaded a printer to issue some of his early poems in a small pamphlet. It was called *Tamerlane and Other Poems*, and the title page said simply "By a Bostonian."

Poe's money was soon gone, and he enlisted in the Army under the name of Edgar A. Perry. In his two years in the Army, he rose to be regimental sergeant major. But he wanted to become an officer, thinking that such advancement would restore him to Allan's favor. After the death of Mrs. Allan in 1829, Poe and Allan were temporarily reconciled. With Allan's help Poe was granted an honorable discharge from the Army. He then sought an appointment to the United States Military Academy at West Point, New York.

Poe waited for more than a year. In the meantime he lived in Baltimore, Maryland, with his father's widowed sister, Maria Clemm, and her young daughter, Virginia. While there he published another volume of poetry, *Al Aaraaf, Tamerlane, and Minor Poems* (1829). On July 1,

1830, he was sworn in as a West Point cadet. He hated the discipline and the restraint of the school. When John Allan married again, Poe lost all chance of becoming his heir. He deliberately neglected his classes and duties and was expelled after eight months.

For the next four years Poe struggled to earn a living as a writer. He returned to Mrs. Clemm's home and submitted stories to magazines. His first success came in 1833, when he entered a short-story contest and won a prize of $50 for the story "MS. Found in a Bottle." By 1835 he was the editor of the *Southern Literary Messenger*. He married his cousin Virginia, who was only 13, and Mrs. Clemm stayed with the couple. The Poes had no children.

Poe's stories, poems, and criticism in the magazine soon attracted attention, and he looked for wider opportunities. From 1837 to 1839 he tried free-lance writing in New York City and Philadelphia but earned very little. Again he tried editing (1839–42). His work was praised, but he was paid little. His efforts to organize his own magazine were unsuccessful. For the next two years he turned again to free-lance writing.

Many of his best stories were written as part of his editorial work. Even those he sold for a fee rarely brought him more than $100 each, but they gave him great publicity. Some of these were: "The Narrative of Arthur Gordon Pym" (1838); "The Fall of the House of Usher" (1839); *Tales of the Grotesque and Arabesque* (appeared 1839; dated 1840); "The Murders in the Rue Morgue" (1841), considered the first detective story; and "The Gold Bug" (1843). During this time his wife showed symptoms of tuberculosis.

In 1844 Poe and his family moved to New York City. There he wrote the "Balloon Hoax" for the *Sun*, and became subeditor of the *New York Mirror* under N.P. Willis. By now Poe was well known in literary circles, and the publication of *The Raven and Other Poems* and a selection of his tales, both in 1845, enhanced his reputation. That same year he became editor of the *Broadway Journal*, a short-lived weekly, in which he republished most of his short stories. The Poes lived in a cottage in Fordham (now in the borough of the Bronx). There Poe wrote for *Godey's Lady's Book* gossipy sketches about personalities of the day, which led to a libel suit. The couple was comfortable for a time, but his wife soon became sicker. Poe also grew weaker and became more dissipated. During the winter of 1846–47 they had little food or fuel. Virginia Poe died on January 30, 1847.

After his wife's death Poe became increasingly depressed and erratic. He courted various women in a vain attempt to find solace for the loss of his wife. His lecture "Eureka," a transcendental explanation of the universe hailed as a masterpiece by some critics and as nonsense by others, was published in 1848. In 1849 he became engaged to a childhood sweetheart, who by then was a wealthy Richmond widow. After making wedding plans, he set out for New York City from Richmond but disappeared in Baltimore. He was found five days after he disappeared and was very near death. He died without regaining full consciousness four days later on October 7, 1849. Poe was buried in Baltimore.

For more than a century speculation persisted that Poe had died of alcohol poisoning. Then, in 1996, Dr. R. Michael Benitez, an assistant professor of medicine at the University of Maryland, concluded in an article published in the Maryland Medical Journal that written accounts of the author's last days suggest that he displayed "all the features of encephalitic rabies." Poe was found delirious in a bar in Baltimore four days before his death. He was taken to the hospital in a comatose state but awoke the next day. For three more days he suffered hallucinations, fits, amnesia, and hydrophobia—all symptoms of rabies. On the fourth day, Poe remained excitable and spastic until he fell into unconsciousness and died. Death in cases of rabies infection normally occurs within three to five days of the appearance of symptoms. Benitez' study provided the first logical explanation for Poe's death. Previous speculation that he died as a result of acute intoxication had been approached with great skepticism by Poe scholars, who pointed out that, as an adult, Poe was so sensitive to alcohol that he rarely drank.

Poe was the first American author to be widely read outside the United States. His reputation in France, especially, was enhanced by the French poet Charles Baudelaire, who read and translated Poe's works in the 1850s. Poe was elected to the United States Hall of Fame in 1910. Since then his reputation in literature has been secure.

# MARCEL PROUST

(b. 1871—d. 1922)

The French novelist Marcel Proust had one of the most original styles in literature. His massive work, *In Search of Lost Time*, is an autobiographical novel told psychologically and allegorically, often in the stream-of-consciousness form. It has had a wide influence. It introduced a new depth of character analysis as well as an unmatched view of French society in the late 19th and early 20th centuries. The novel's title in French is *À la recherche du temps perdu*, and it has also been translated into English as *Remembrance of Things Past*.

Proust was born on July 10, 1871, in Auteuil, a suburb of Paris. His father was a French Roman Catholic physician, and his mother came from a successful Jewish family. From the time he was nine, Proust suffered severely from asthma. His studies at the Lycée Condorcet were interrupted from time to time by his illness, but he wrote for school magazines and was a good student. He enjoyed the *Memoirs* of Louis de St-Simon and decided that he would be the one to chronicle modern French society as St-Simon had portrayed court life during the reign of Louis XIV.

In 1889 he registered for military service and served in the army in Orléans for a year. His father suggested that Proust pursue a diplomatic career, but instead he studied law, philosophy, and literature. During this time Proust became a member of Paris' most fashionable society. He entertained lavishly and counted among his friends members of the most elite social circles.

A book of Proust's short stories, poems, and sketches with a preface by Anatole France was published in 1896, though some of its contents had appeared previously. It was called *Pleasures and Regrets*. Proust became involved with the Dreyfus affair of 1897–99 when he helped organize petitions on behalf of Alfred Dreyfus, who had been unjustly imprisoned as a spy. Proust's experience in this matter heightened his disillusionment with society, and this played a large role in his writing. Proust published translations of two works by John Ruskin and stylistic imitations of several well-known French writers in the magazine *Le Figaro*. He began work on his autobiographical novel *Jean Santeuil* in 1895 but never finished it; it was published after his death, in 1952.

Proust's father died in 1903, and his mother died two years later. Proust was grief-stricken and lived the rest of his life as a recluse in his home on Boulevard Haussmann. His parents had left him financially independent, so Proust was able to concentrate on his major novel. *In Search of Lost Time* is a multivolume work based on Proust's own life and told as an allegorical search for truth. He finished the first volume and was forced to pay for its publication himself because it was refused by all of Paris' major publishing houses. *Swann's Way* appeared in 1914. *Within a Budding Grove*, published in 1919, won the prestigious Goncourt Prize. *The Guermantes Way* and *Sodom and Gomorrah* were published in 1921. Proust died of pneumonia on November 18, 1922. The last parts of the novel were published posthumously: *The Captive* in 1923, *The Fugitive* in 1925, and *Time Regained* in 1927.

# PHILIP ROTH

(b. 1932—d. )

U.S. novelist. Philip Roth was a celebrated author of the middle and late 20th century. His writing was marked by thinly veiled autobiography and a sardonic sense of humor about Jewish life in the United States. Among his popular and award-winning novels were *Portnoy's Complaint*, *The Counterlife*, and *Operation Shylock*.

Philip Roth was born to Herman and Bess Roth on March 19, 1933 in Newark, New Jersey. Roth recalled his childhood in the middle class, predominantly Jewish neighborhood as being filled with a constant hum of activity and a feeling of community among the families of second-generation immigrants.

Philip attended Chancellor Avenue Elementary School and went to Hebrew school three nights a week. At Weequahic High School, he was known as an intelligent, popular boy with a quick sarcastic wit. Roth's impressions of his childhood and adolescence were immortalized in later

Philip Roth, 1993.

novels—he even went so far as to mention some of the places and people by name.

Roth began his college career at Newark College, later went to Rutgers University, and eventually graduated from Bucknell University in 1954. He earned a master's degree at the University of Chicago in 1955. He enlisted in the Army in 1955, worked in the Public Information Office in Washington, D.C., and was later discharged because of a back injury. His stories began to appear in 1956, when he began teaching and working toward a Ph.D. at the University of Chicago.

Roth's first book, *Goodbye, Columbus, and Five Short Stories*, was published in 1959. The collection provided a first glimpse of some defining characteristics of Roth's work: his biting humor and exploration of what it meant to be Jewish in the United States. *Goodbye, Columbus* won the National Book Award for fiction in 1959.

For the next ten years, Roth taught creative writing at the University of Chicago, the University of Iowa, and Princeton University while continuing to work on his own writing. His first novel, *Letting Go*, was published in 1962, followed by *When She Was Good* in 1967. The publication of *Portnoy's Complaint* in 1969 brought a storm of criticism from the Jewish community. The protagonist, Portnoy, is a guilt-ridden observer of the Jews living in the United States after World War II. He observes that Jews are not only victimized by bigots but also by other Jews, and presents them both making and breaking stereotypes. Roth's intensely personal criticisms of the Jewish community led some to charge him with anti-Semitism.

Perhaps in response, Roth created an alter ego, Nathan Zuckerman, for a series that began with the publication of *My Life as a Man* in 1974 and continued with *The Ghost Writer* (1979), *Zuckerman Unbound* (1981), *The Anatomy Lesson* (1983), and *The Counterlife* (1986), which won the National Book Critics Circle award in 1987. During this very prolific period, Roth also wrote *Our Gang* (1971), *The Breast* (1972), *The Great American Novel* (1973) and *The Professor of Desire* (1977), as well as several essays and critical works.

Roth's work continued to walk the thin line between fact and fiction, and in some cases ignored the line completely. In the mid-1970s he became involved with actress Claire Bloom, whom he portrayed—often unflatteringly—in many of his novels. Their 17-year relationship ended after three years of marriage, and Bloom wrote her own book, *Leaving a Doll's House*, in which she described their relationship as tortured.

With the publication of *The Facts: A Novelist's Autobiography* in 1988, Roth directly confronted his critics' claims of inserting too much of himself into his books. The result was confusion over whether the book truly presented "the facts" or was just more fiction. Nathan Zuckerman appeared at the end to converse with the author and chastise him for his false presentation of his life. Roth himself seemed to be unsure of where fact ended and fiction began. *Deception: A Novel* (1990), *Patrimony: A True Story* (1991), *Operation Shylock: A Confession* (1993), and *Sabbath's Theater* (1995) only furthered the mystery of who Philip Roth was apart from his "fictional self-legends." Nathan Zuckerman made a return appearance in *American Pastoral*, published in 1997.

Whatever the relationship to Roth's real life, his novels were well received by the public and by critics. *Patrimony* won the National Book Critics Circle award in 1992, *Operation Shylock* won the PEN/Faulkner Award for Fiction and *Time* magazine's Best American Novel in 1993, and *Sabbath's Theater* won the National Book award for fiction in 1995. Despite all of this success, however, Roth claimed in an interview that "with each new project I feel like, and I am, a clumsy beginner."

## J.K. ROWLING

(b. 1965—d. )

British author J.K. Rowling captured the imagination of children and adults alike with her best-selling series of books about Harry Potter, a young sorcerer in training. The books were critically acclaimed as well as wildly popular and were credited with generating a new interest in reading among children, the books' intended audience.

Joanne Kathleen Rowling was born on July 31, 1965, in Yate, near Bristol, England. She grew up in Chepstow, Gwent, Wales, where she wrote her first story at the age of six. After graduating from the University of Exeter in 1986, Rowling began working for Amnesty International in

London. The idea for the Harry Potter stories came to her during a train ride in 1990, and she began writing the magic adventure while sitting in cafés and pubs. In the early 1990s she traveled to Portugal to teach English as a foreign language, but after a brief marriage and the birth of her daughter, she returned to the United Kingdom, settling in Edinburgh, Scotland. Living on public assistance between stints as a French teacher, she continued to write, often on scraps of paper and napkins.

After being rejected by several publishers, Rowling's first manuscript was purchased by Bloomsbury Children's Books in 1996. *Harry Potter and the Philosopher's Stone* (1997), which was known in the United States as *Harry Potter and the Sorcerer's Stone*, was an immediate success. Featuring vivid descriptions and an imaginative story line, it followed the adventures of the unlikely hero Harry Potter, a lonely orphan who

J.K. Rowling, 2005.

discovers that he is actually a wizard and enrolls in the Hogwarts School of Witchcraft and Wizardry. The book received numerous awards, including the British Book Award. All six succeeding volumes—*Harry Potter and the Chamber of Secrets* (1998), *Harry Potter and the Prisoner of Azkaban* (1999), *Harry Potter and the Goblet of Fire* (2000), *Harry Potter and the Order of the Phoenix* (2003), *Harry Potter and the Half-Blood Prince* (2005), and *Harry Potter and the Deathly Hallows* (2007), which was the seventh and final book in the series—also were best-sellers, available in more than 200 countries and some 60 languages. In 2001 the companion books *Fantastic Beasts & Where to Find Them* and *Quidditch Through the Ages* were published, with the proceeds going to charity. A movie based on the first Harry Potter book, released in November 2001, broke box-office records for its first-weekend gross in both the United Kingdom and North America. A series of sequels followed. Rowling was appointed an Officer of the British Empire in 2001.

# SALMAN RUSHDIE

(b. 1947—d. )

Anglo-Indian novelist Salman Rushdie was condemned to death by leading Iranian Muslim clerics in 1989 for allegedly blaspheming Islam in his novel *The Satanic Verses*. His case became the focus of an international controversy.

Ahmed Salman Rushdie was born on June 19, 1947, in Bombay (now Mumbai), India. He was the son of a prosperous Muslim businessman. Rushdie was educated at Rugby School and the University of Cambridge in England, receiving a master's degree in history in 1968. After university, he worked in London as an advertising copywriter, and he published his first novel *Grimus* in 1975. His next novel was *Midnight's Children* (1981), an allegory about modern India. It was an unexpected success that won him international recognition and the Booker prize. Like Rushdie's subsequent fiction, *Midnight's Children* is an allegorical fable that examines historical and philosophical issues by means of surreal characters, brooding humor, and melodramatic prose.

Salman Rushdie in 1993.

Rushdie's novel *Shame* (1983) was based on contemporary politics in Pakistan and also became popular, but *The Satanic Verses* (1988), his fourth novel, encountered a different reception. Some of the adventures in this book depict a character modeled after the Prophet Muhammad and portray both him and his transcription of the Koran (Qur'an) in a way that drew criticism from Muslim community leaders in Britain, who denounced the novel as blasphemous. In 1989 the spiritual leader of revolutionary Iran, Ayatollah Ruhollah Khomeini, publicly condemned the book and issued a *fatwa* (legal opinion) against Rushdie. The Iranian government offered a bounty to anyone who would execute him, so Rushdie retreated into hiding. In 1998 the Iranian government finally announced that it would no longer seek to enforce its *fatwa* against him.

Meanwhile, Rushdie continued to publish his writings, and in 1990 he embraced Islam and halted the paperback edition and further translations of *The Satanic Verses*. He also wrote a collection of essays and criticism, *Imaginary Homelands* (1991); a children's book, *Haroun and the Sea of Stories* (1990); a collection of short stories, *East, West* (1994); a collection of essays, *Step Across This Line* (2002); and several novels, *The Moor's Last Sigh (1995), The Ground Beneath Her Feet (1999), Fury (2001), Shalimar the Clown (2005); The Enchantress of Florence (2008);* and *Luka and the Fire of Life* (2010).

The British government made him a knight in 2007. Rushdie won two special Booker prizes, voted on by the public, in 1993 and 2008, given in honor of the prize's 25th and 40th anniversaries, respectively.

## J.D. SALINGER

(b. 1919—d. 2010)

Although he is one of the most widely read authors in the English language, J.D. Salinger successfully kept himself out of the public eye for most of his career. His preference for seclusion made his life a matter of speculation among fans and his literary output a subject of controversy among critics.

Jerome David Salinger was born in New York City on January 1, 1919. After studying at Columbia and New York universities, he turned to writing. His first short story appeared in *Story* magazine in 1940. After service in World War II his stories appeared regularly in the *New Yorker* magazine. Major recognition and a large following came with his novel, *The Catcher in the Rye*, published in 1951. This touching and humorous story about a rebellious teenager became a cult favorite among students. It was followed by *Nine Stories* (1953), *Franny and Zooey* (1961), and *Raise High the Roof Beam, Carpenters; and Seymour: An Introduction* (1963). The last two volumes contain stories about the Glass family.

Altogether Salinger produced 13 short stories and one novel. Some of the stories made use of his wartime experiences, as in "For Esmé—with Love and Squalor" (1950). "A Perfect Day for Bananafish" (1948) concerns the despair of veteran Seymour Glass. Salinger seemed at his best in dramatizing the lives of children. His work concerns the lost innocence of childhood. Salinger died January 27, 2010, in Cornish, New Hampshire.

# WILLIAM SHAKESPEARE

(b. 1564—d. 1616)

William Shakespeare was born in Stratford-upon-Avon, England, in 1564. This was the sixth year of the reign of Queen Elizabeth I. He was christened on April 26 of that year. The day of his birth is unknown. It has long been celebrated on April 23, the feast of St. George.

He was the third child and oldest son of John and Mary Arden Shakespeare. Two sisters, Joan and Margaret, died before he was born. The other children were Gilbert, a second Joan, Anne, Richard, and Edmund. Only the second Joan outlived William.

Shakespeare's father was a tanner and glovemaker. He was an alderman of Stratford for years. He also served a term as high bailiff, or mayor. Toward the end of his life John Shakespeare lost most of his money. When he died in 1601, he left William only a little real estate. Not much is known about Mary Shakespeare, except that she came from a wealthier family than her husband.

Stratford-upon-Avon is in Warwickshire, called the heart of England. In Shakespeare's day it was well farmed and heavily wooded. The town itself was prosperous and progressive.

The town was proud of its grammar school. Young Shakespeare went to it, although when or for how long is not known. He may have been a pupil there between his 7th and 13th years. His studies must have been mainly in Latin. The schooling was probably good. All four schoolmasters at the school during Shakespeare's boyhood were graduates of Oxford University.

In 1582, when he was 18, he married Anne Hathaway. She was from Shottery, a village a mile (1.6 kilometers) from Stratford. Anne was seven or eight years older than Shakespeare. From this difference in their ages, a story arose that they were unhappy together. Their first daughter, Susanna, was born in 1583. In 1585 a twin boy and girl, Hamnet and Judith, were born.

What Shakespeare did between 1583 and 1592 is not known. Various stories are told. He may have taught school, worked in a lawyer's office, served on a rich man's estate, or traveled with a company of actors. One famous story says that about 1584 he and some friends were caught poaching on the estate of Sir Thomas Lucy of Carlecote, near Warwick, and were forced to leave town. A less likely story is that he was in London in 1588. There he was supposed to have held horses for theater patrons and later to have worked in the theaters as a page.

By 1592, however, Shakespeare was definitely in London and was already recognized as an actor and playwright. He was then 28 years old. In that year Robert Greene, a playwright, accused him of borrowing from the plays of others.

Between 1592 and 1594, plague kept the London theaters closed most of the time. During these years Shakespeare wrote his earliest sonnets and two long narrative poems, *Venus and Adonis* and *The Rape of Lucrece*. Both were printed by Richard Field, a boyhood friend from Stratford. They were well received and helped establish him as a poet.

Until 1598 Shakespeare's theater work was confined to a district northeast of London. This was outside the city walls, in the parish of Shoreditch. Located there were two playhouses, the Theatre and the Curtain. Both were managed by James Burbage, whose son Richard Burbage was Shakespeare's friend and the greatest tragic actor of his day.

Up to 1596 Shakespeare lived near these theaters in Bishopsgate, where the North Road entered the city. Sometime between 1596 and 1599, he moved across the Thames River to a district called Bankside. There, two theaters, the Rose and the Swan, had been built by Philip Henslowe. He was James Burbage's chief competitor in London as a theater manager. The Burbages also moved to this district in 1598 and built the famous Globe Theatre. Its sign showed Atlas supporting the world. Shakespeare was associated with the Globe Theatre for the rest of his active life. He owned shares in it, which brought him much money.

Meanwhile, in 1597, Shakespeare had bought New Place, the largest house in Stratford. During the next three years he bought other property in Stratford and in London. The year before, his father, probably at Shakespeare's suggestion, applied for and was granted a coat of arms. It bore the motto *Non sanz droict*—Not without right. From this time on, Shakespeare could write "Gentleman" after his name. This meant much to him, for in his day actors were classed legally with criminals and vagrants.

William Shakespeare, detail of an oil painting attributed to John Taylor.

Shakespeare's name first appeared on the title pages of his printed plays in 1598. In the same year Francis Meres, in *Palladis Tamia: Wit's Treasury*, praised him as a poet and dramatist. Meres's comments on 12 of Shakespeare's plays showed that Shakespeare's genius was recognized in his own time.

Shakespeare's first period of writing was his apprenticeship. Between the ages of 26 and 30 he was learning his craft. He imitated Roman comedy and tragedy and followed the styles of the playwrights who came just before him. He may have collaborated with Christopher Marlowe and others. The Senecan tragedy, or "tragedy of blood," was in style at this time. Shakespeare too wrote plays in this fashion. Later he wrote chronicle, or history, plays when these became popular.

His second period is highlighted by *Romeo and Juliet*, *The Merchant of Venice*, and *Henry IV*. He had mastered his art. He tried the comedy of local middle-class people only once, in *The Merry Wives of Windsor*. His heart was not in it. His favorite style was the romantic comedy. During this period he shows ease, power, and maturity. The plays are generally sunny and full of joyous poetry.

With *Hamlet*, written in about 1601, his third period begins. For eight years he probed the problem of evil in the world. At times he reached an almost desperate pessimism. Even the comedies of this period are bitter.

In his fourth and last period Shakespeare used a new form. It was the tragicomedy, or dramatic romance. In his hands the tragicomedy is calm, sober, and quietly lovely. *The Tempest* is perhaps the most beautiful and serene of all his plays.

Queen Elizabeth I died in 1603. King James I followed her to the throne. Shakespeare's theatrical company was taken under the king's patronage and called the King's Company. Shakespeare and the other actors were made officers of the royal household. The theatrical company was the most successful of its time. Before it was the King's Company, it had been known as the Earl of Derby's and the Lord Chamberlain's. In 1608 the company acquired the Blackfriars Theatre. This was a smaller and more aristocratic theater than the Globe. Thereafter the company alternated between the two playhouses.

Plays by Shakespeare were also performed at the royal court and in the castles of the nobles. After 1603 Shakespeare probably acted little, although he was still a good actor. His favorite roles seem to have been old Adam in *As You Like It* and the Ghost in *Hamlet*. In 1607, when he was 43, he may have suffered a serious physical breakdown. In the same year his older daughter Susanna married John Hall, a doctor. The next year Shakespeare's first grandchild, Elizabeth, was born. Also in 1607 his brother Edmund, also a London actor, died at the age of 27.

Shakespeare retired from his theater work in 1610 and returned to Stratford. His friends from London visited him. In 1613 the Globe Theatre burned. He lost much money in it, but he was still wealthy. He shared in the building of the new Globe. A few months before the fire he bought as an investment a house in the fashionable Blackfriars district of London.

On April 23, 1616, Shakespeare died at the age of 52. This date is according to the Old Style, or Julian, calendar of his time. The New Style, or Gregorian, calendar date is May 3, 1616. He was buried in the chancel of the Church of the Holy Trinity in Stratford.

# GEORGE BERNARD SHAW

(b. 1856—d. 1950)

"I have been dinning into the public head that I am an extraordinarily witty, brilliant and clever man. That is now part of the public opinion of England; and no power in heaven or on Earth will ever change it." George Bernard Shaw wrote this about himself in 1898. He was then 42 years old. A tall, thin, red-bearded man, he was already well known in London, England, as a critic of music, art, and drama. He was an influential socialist speaker, and he had written plays that attacked the accepted ideas of his time.

George Bernard Shaw—often referred to by his initials—was born in Dublin, Ireland, on July 26, 1856, to an Irish Protestant family. His father had a small wholesale business but drank heavily and neglected his affairs. Shaw's mother was a cold, humorless woman whose main interest was music. Eventually she and her husband were separated.

His mother's interest in music offered her and her son a means of escape from this situation. She became acquainted with a musician named George John Vandaleur Lee, and in association with him she filled her house with other musicians. Shaw heard so much music during this period of his life that he developed a deep appreciation for classical music.

Shaw's formal education did not last long. He was tutored by his uncle, then attended day schools, in which he was "near or at the bottom" of his class. By the age of 15 he had become a clerk in a land agent's office. He was a good worker, but he saw no future for himself in office work. His mother and sister had left his father in Dublin and moved to London, and in 1876 he joined them there.

He spent his days at the British Museum reading room, writing several novels—all failures—and studying. During the evenings he began to attend lectures and debates, and he developed into an effective orator. He joined the Fabian Society in 1884 and became one of its most active members. In 1885 Shaw was given a job as a book reviewer for the *Pall Mall Gazette*. This was followed by several other jobs as a critic of books, art, or theater for various periodicals.

Shaw's first play, *Widowers' Houses*, was performed in 1892. This was the first of many plays, nearly all successful. His main purpose as a dramatist was to shock people out of conventional, hidebound ways of thinking. His view of his work was reflected in the title of his collection *Plays: Pleasant and Unpleasant*, published in 1898. *Mrs. Warren's Profession*, which was not produced until 1902 because of censorship, was included in this collection. Shaw labeled such plays as unpleasant because "their dramatic power is used to force the spectator to face unpleasant facts."

The play concerns the inability of one of the characters to accept the fact that her mother, Mrs. Warren, gained her fortune through prostitution. Mrs. Warren is the most conventional character in the play, and she defends her life with an attack on the society that rewards vice and oppresses virtue.

Among Shaw's many plays are *Arms and the Man* (1894), *Candida* (1897), *Caesar and Cleopatra* (1901), *Man and Superman* (1905), *Major Barbara* (1905), *Pygmalion* (1913), and *Saint Joan* (1923). Shaw also published many essays, including "The Intelligent Woman's Guide to Socialism and Capitalism" (1928).

In 1898 Shaw married Charlotte Payne-Townshend. They had no children, and Mrs. Shaw died in 1943. His correspondence over the years with the actresses Ellen Terry and Mrs. Patrick Campbell was widely publicized. In 1925 he won the Nobel Prize in Literature. Shaw died in Ayot St. Lawrence, Hertfordshire, on November 2, 1950.

## MARY WOLLSTONECRAFT SHELLEY

(b. 1797—d. 1851)

The English Romantic writer Mary Wollstonecraft Shelley is remembered primarily for her classic Gothic novel *Frankenstein*. The book gave birth to what was to become one of the Western world's best-known monsters.

The only daughter of social philosopher William Godwin and feminist Mary Wollstonecraft, Mary Wollstonecraft Godwin was born on

Mary Wollstonecraft Shelley in an oil portrait by Richard Rothwell.

August 30, 1797, in London, England. She met the young poet Percy Bysshe Shelley in the spring of 1814 and eloped with him to France in July of that year. The couple were married in 1816, after Shelley's first wife had committed suicide. Mary Shelley apparently came as near as any woman could to meeting Percy Shelley's requirements for his life's partner: "one who can feel poetry and understand philosophy." After her husband's death in 1822, she returned to England and devoted herself to publicizing Shelley's writings and to educating their only surviving child, Percy Florence Shelley. She published her late husband's *Posthumous Poems* (1824) and edited his *Poetical Works* (1839), with long and invaluable notes, and his prose works. Her *Journal* and letters are a rich source of biographical information.

Mary Shelley's best-known novel is *Frankenstein, or The Modern Prometheus* (1818), in which she narrates the dreadful consequences that arise after a scientist has artificially created a human being. The novel belongs to the contemporary Gothic school, which used horror as its primary device. It offered fertile ground for such typically Romantic themes as the relationship of science to humanity and the embodied alter ego. The monster in this novel inspired a similar creature in several famous U.S. horror films of the 1930s.

Mary Shelley wrote several other novels, such as *Valperga* (1823), *The Fortunes of Perkin Warbeck* (1830), *Lodore* (1835), and *Falkner* (1837), but *The Last Man* (1826), an account of the future destruction of the human race by a plague, is still ranked as her best work. Her travel book *History of a Six Weeks' Tour* (1817) recounts the continental tour she and Shelley took in 1814 following their elopement and then describes their summer near Geneva in 1816. Mary Shelley died in London on February 1, 1851.

## GERTRUDE STEIN

(b. 1874—d. 1946)

Although she fancied herself a genius and published a number of books and plays, Gertrude Stein is remembered best for the talented people who visited her in Paris, France. She and her brother, art critic Leo Stein, were among the first to appreciate and collect the works of such major artists as Pablo Picasso, Paul Cézanne, and Henri Matisse. She also befriended and encouraged such expatriate American writers as Ernest Hemingway and Sherwood Anderson.

Stein was born on February 3, 1874, in Allegheny, Pennsylvania. She grew up in Oakland, California, and attended Radcliffe College in Cambridge, Massachusetts, and, for a time, the medical school at Johns Hopkins University in Baltimore, Maryland. In 1903 she joined her brother in Paris. Except for time spent in the French village of Culoz during World War II, Paris was her home for the rest of her life.

Her first book, *Three Lives*, was published in 1909 and describes the lives of three working-class women. Her best-known book is *The Autobiography of Alice B. Toklas* (1933). Although the name in the title is that of Stein's friend and companion for many years, the book is by and about Stein herself. Toklas's actual autobiography, *What Is Remembered* (1963), appeared long after Stein's death. Stein also wrote the librettos for two operas by Virgil Thomson—*Four Saints in Three Acts* (1934) and *The Mother of Us All* (1947). Her last book, *Brewsie and Willie* (1946), is about the American servicemen who visited her during the war. Stein died on July 27, 1946, in Paris.

# JOHN STEINBECK

(b. 1902—d. 1968)

Winner of the 1962 Nobel Prize in Literature, the American author John Steinbeck is best remembered for his novel *The Grapes of Wrath*. Steinbeck's story of a family of farm workers migrating from Oklahoma to California describes the hopelessness of the Great Depression era.

John Ernst Steinbeck was born on February 27, 1902, in Salinas, California He took classes at Stanford University for several years but left without a degree. He worked as a laborer to support himself while he wrote. Steinbeck's first novel was published in 1929, but it was not until the publication of *Tortilla Flat* in 1935 that he attained critical and popular acclaim.

He followed this success with *In Dubious Battle* (1936) and *Of Mice and Men* (1937). *The Grapes of Wrath* (1939) earned for Steinbeck a Pulitzer Prize. In these works Steinbeck's proletarian themes are expressed through his portrayal of the inarticulate, dispossessed laborers who populate his American landscape. Both *Of Mice and Men* and *The Grapes of Wrath* were made into motion pictures.

In 1943 Steinbeck traveled to North Africa and Italy as a war correspondent. Some of his later works include *Cannery Row (1945), The Pearl (1947), East of Eden (1952), The Winter of Our Discontent (1961),* and *Travels with Charley* (1962). He also wrote several motion-picture scripts, including adaptations of two of his shorter works—*The Pearl* and *The Red Pony*. Steinbeck died in New York City on December 20, 1968.

# JONATHAN SWIFT

(b. 1667—d. 1745)

When Jonathan Swift wrote *Gulliver's Travels*, he intended it as a satire on all of humankind. He proposed, in his own words, "to vex the world rather than divert it." Instead, people enjoyed his story and gave it to children to read. Today most readers know this quite ferocious indictment of human nature only as an amusing tale for children.

Jonathan Swift was born on November 30, 1667, in Dublin, Ireland. His parents were English. His grandfather, a vicar, had supported the Royalists during the English Civil War and had lost all he owned.

Born a few months after his father's death, Swift was dependent upon an uncle who was, the boy thought, ungenerous. At the age of six Swift was separated from his mother. She went back to live in England while he was sent to Kilkenny School, considered the Eton of Ireland. He was admitted to Trinity College, Dublin, in 1682. After earning his bachelor's degree four years later, he remained at the college for three more years, not quite long enough for a higher degree. He spent much of his time reading for his own pleasure, stayed away from lectures and chapel, and amused himself with friends in town.

The Revolution of 1688 made the English living in Ireland feel insecure, and Jonathan Swift left college the following year to travel to the safety of England. Through his uncle he was introduced to Sir William Temple, a retired Anglo-Irish statesman. Swift became a secretary to Temple and lived at his house off and on for ten years.

Although Temple was kind to him on the whole, Swift could not forget that he was a dependent. His chief comfort in his painful situation was his friendship with a child, Esther Johnson, whose mother was Temple's housekeeper. When Swift first met Esther she was only 8 years old—14 years younger than he. He taught her to read and write, and throughout her life she was his closest friend. After her death she was known to the world as Stella, a nickname Swift gave her. They may have been secretly married as early as 1716, but they probably never lived together as husband and wife.

During the first years with Temple, Swift wrote a few poems that the poet Dryden, Swift's cousin, is said to have told him were not good—as they were not. Bitterly Swift turned from writing poetry, which he did not think of as a profession. He went to Ireland in 1694 and entered the Church of England. He was first sent to a rural parish near Belfast. This bored him, and he was soon back with Temple. But now Swift knew he had a profession, and he felt assured about his future. Between 1696 and

1697 he wrote his first important satires, *A Tale of a Tub* and *The Battle of the Books*. He did not publish them, however, until 1704.

Temple's death in 1699 caused Swift to return to Ireland, and Stella soon followed him. Again Swift was assigned to a small parish in the country.

Swift was free to leave his parish in the curate's charge, and he spent a good deal of his time in Dublin. He also made long visits to London.

What took him to London was a mission from the Irish church to obtain benefits from Queen Anne. What kept him there were both his duties as a lobbyist and his attempts to get a higher appointment in the church. There was also his friendship with the wits of London, where *A Tale of a Tub* made him quickly famous. Joseph Addison and Richard Steele were his close friends. He wrote for the *Tatler* and took part in humorous hoaxes. Like Addison and Steele, he was a Whig in politics.

In 1710 Swift, up to that time a Whig, went over to the Tories, chiefly because he thought they showed more concern for the church. This led to his employment by the newly seated Tory ministry. The chief aim of the Tories was to end the long war with France. The war, supported by the Whigs, was being waged by their great general, the duke of Marlborough. The Tory ministers set themselves to destroy Whig power, oust Marlborough, and bring peace. They used Swift to arouse public opinion against the Whigs by his writings.

In the Tory *Examiner* and in pamphlets and verse Swift carried on a vigorous campaign against Marlborough for his greed and against the Whigs for their refusal to view the interests of Britain as a whole. In all this Swift wrote anonymously.

Alienated by politics from Addison and Steele, Swift made new literary friends among the Tories: the witty and spiteful Alexander Pope; John Gay, author of *The Beggar's Opera*; and John Arbuthnot, physician to Queen Anne. With some others they formed the Scriblerus Club. Together they planned to write the burlesque memoirs of the imaginary Martinus Scriblerus, ridiculing false learning. Although this project was barely begun and outlined, it was the seed of *Gulliver's Travels*.

Marlborough was recalled, and the war ended with the Treaty of Utrecht in 1713, but the Tory ministry did not last. After the queen's death in 1714 the Whigs regained their power. Swift had hoped he might become a bishop. But he had too many enemies, and his friends did no more than make him dean of St. Patrick's Cathedral in Dublin.

During these years of daily association with the great, Swift sent Stella in Dublin a day-by-day account of everything he did. This *Journal to Stella*, written with no thought of publication, is a fascinating record not only of Swift's life but also of London society and politics in Queen Anne's reign. It remains one of the great diaries of English literature.

Although Swift was to become a champion of the Irish, he returned to Ireland as to a place of exile. London had been the scene of his successes. In Ireland he was out of the world in which he had come to feel at home. For ten years Swift took almost no interest in anything. His one confidante was Stella.

When he emerged from his silence he again attacked the Whigs, but now as Englishmen misgoverning Ireland. In 1729 he published the most terrible of his satiric pamphlets, *A Modest Proposal*—that the Irish poor raise their children as food for the tables of the wealthy, particularly their English landlords.

After 1720 Swift again took up the Scriblerus memoirs, and by 1725 he had finished *Gulliver's Travels*. The next year he took the manuscript to London. Because of the political satire in it, the book appeared anonymously.

After a second visit to London, in 1727, Swift remained in Ireland. Stella died in 1728, and in spite of devoted friends Swift was very lonely. He suffered from attacks of deafness and dizziness, and for the last three years of his life some people thought that he was insane. He died on October 19, 1745, and was buried in St. Patrick's Cathedral beside Stella.

When *Gulliver's Travels* was published in 1726, the author's name did not appear on the book. The title page read "Travels into several remote Nations of the World, by Lemuel Gulliver…" Many people accepted this as fact. Travel books of the time told many tales that were no more strange than the imaginary adventures of Gulliver. One sea captain even claimed that he knew Captain Gulliver well. Other readers condemned the book as full of exaggerations.

Although it became one of the most famous books for children, it was not written for children. It was savage satire aimed at the human race. The tiny Lilliputians are vain, malicious, and bloodthirsty. The king and the court of Lilliput are a parody of the English king and court.

The giants of Brobdingnag are amiable, but commonplace and insensitive. Laputa is full of the foolish philosophers and scientists whom Swift despised. The Houyhnhnms are horses who use degraded men, Yahoos, as men use horses elsewhere. Looking at mankind through the eyes of horses, Swift sees people as vicious, greedy, and ignorant.

From its first appearance *Gulliver's Travels* delighted its readers instead of shocking them. In spite of his bitterness, Swift took a dry delight in making his narrative sound real even when it was fantastic. Children could enjoy the marvelous adventures of a traveler among pygmies and giants, on a flying island, and in a country where horses talk. *Gulliver's Travels* soon became a children's classic.

A large part of what Swift wrote is made up of pamphlets on political or ecclesiastical affairs and must be read in the light of history. But *A Tale of a Tub*, a satire on false religion, and *The Battle of the Books*, a burlesque of literary controversy (both published in 1704), are still read for their comic ridicule of human folly. *Drapier's Letters* (1724), written to expose a minor scandal in the government of Ireland by the English, lifts the issue to something universal—the human rights of men against tyrants. The *Journal to Stella* is a brilliant picture of a brilliant age.

# HENRY DAVID THOREAU

(b. 1817—d. 1862)

If the movement called New England Transcendentalism stood for the individual as rebel against the established orders of society, then Henry David Thoreau was its foremost representative. He was a man unto himself who looked at society and government and found them lacking in nearly every respect. His friend Ralph Waldo Emerson said of him: "He was bred to no profession; he never married; he lived alone; he never went to church; he never voted; he refused to pay a tax to the state; he ate no flesh; he drank no wine; he never knew the use of tobacco; and, though a naturalist, he used neither trap nor gun."

To a modern observer, Thoreau's life might appear drab and uninteresting. To those who know his writings, however, he is an author of international stature whose words can still move and inspire.

He was born on July 12, 1817, at Concord, Massachusetts, where he spent nearly his whole life. He graduated from Harvard University in 1837 and failed at a teaching job before operating a private school with his brother John from about 1838 until John fell ill in 1841.

Emerson and his family had moved to Concord in 1834, and Thoreau lived at Emerson's home intermittently. It was while there that he decided to devote his life to writing. He rarely worked at anything else except his father's pencil-making business and surveying.

It was restlessness that led him to seek the solitude of Walden Pond, 2 miles (3.2 kilometers) from Concord. He built a small cabin and moved into it on July 4, 1845. He left Walden on September 6, 1847. During this period he wrote *A Week on the Concord and Merrimack Rivers*, published in 1849; composed hundreds of pages in his journal; and executed the first draft of *Walden; or, Life in the Woods* (1854).

During his Walden stay he was forced to spend a night in jail for failure to pay the poll tax. From this experience came a lecture, "Civil Disobedience." The experience marked a turning point. He vowed not to support a government that permitted slavery and waged an imperialist war against Mexico. He helped to free slaves through the Underground Railroad, and, in the fiery abolitionist John Brown, Thoreau found a new hero. His "Plea for Captain John Brown" is among his best works. Thoreau lived only a few years more. He died of tuberculosis on May 6, 1862.

He was an individualist but of a peculiarly American type. "We go westward," he said, "as into the future, with a spirit of enterprise and adventure." Among his other works, published after his death, were *Life Without Principle* (1863), *Excursions* (1863), and *The Maine Woods* (1864).

## J.R.R. TOLKIEN

(b. 1892—d. 1973)

His heroes are rather short, rather stout, and have very furry feet. English author J.R.R. Tolkien's fantastic tales of battles between good and evil, including *The Lord of the Rings* trilogy, made "hobbit" a household word.

John Ronald Reuel Tolkien was born in Bloemfontein, South Africa, on January 3, 1892, and moved at age four with his family to England, where he was educated at Exeter College, Oxford. He was a professor at Oxford from 1925 to 1959 and first gained recognition as a philologist, a person who studies the way language is used in literature. This work led him to help edit a version of the English fable *Sir Gawain and the Green Knight* that was published in 1925.

Tolkien not only studied fables; he created new ones of his own. He invented an imaginary land, Middle Earth, in meticulous detail: its language, its geography, and its exciting history. *The Hobbit; or, There and Back Again*, published in 1937, introduces readers to this special world as its inhabitants—elves, dwarfs, wizards, and the furry-footed hobbit Bilbo Baggins—fight and win against an evil dragon.

This story is continued in The Lord of the Rings trilogy (1954–55), consisting of *The Fellowship of the Ring, The Two Towers*, and *The Return of the King*. These tales became immensely popular in the 1960s, especially among young adults. Another Tolkien book on Middle Earth, *The Silmarillion*, was published four years after his death in Bournemouth, England, on September 2, 1973.

## LEO TOLSTOY

(b. 1828—d. 1910)

The great novels of the Russian writer Leo Tolstoy capture the vastness of the Russian landscape and the complexity of its people. His massive work *War and Peace* (1869) is regarded as a milestone in the development of the Western novel and spread his social and moral ideals to all parts of the world.

Lev Nikolayevich Tolstoy (Tolstoy also spelled Tolstoi) was born in the village of Yasnaya Polyana in Tula province, in the Russian Empire, on September 9 (August 28 according to the calendar being used at the time), 1828. His parents, Count Nikolay Ilich Tolstoy and Princess

Mariya Nikolayevna Volkonskaya, came from distinguished families of the Russian nobility. His mother died before Tolstoy turned two, and his father died in 1837. After his grandmother and an aunt died, Tolstoy and his four siblings were raised by another aunt in western Russia. Despite the constant presence of death, Tolstoy remembered his childhood as happy, and he re-created many of the scenes of his youth in his writings.

Tolstoy was educated at home by tutors before entering the University of Kazan in 1844 as a student of Oriental languages. Poor grades soon forced him to transfer to the less-demanding law faculty, but he found himself interested in literature and ethics. His study of the French philosopher Jean-Jacques Rousseau encouraged his rebellious attitude and greatly influenced his moral, social, and educational beliefs. In 1847 Tolstoy left the university, saying that he had lost faith in religion and prayer.

In 1851, tired of the irresponsible lifestyle he had chosen, Tolstoy accompanied his brother Nikolay, a military officer, to the Caucasus region and then joined the Russian army in 1852. In 1854 he was commissioned an officer and served in the Crimean War until 1856. He used and described his army experiences in many of his stories and novels.

Tolstoy's first published work appeared under a pseudonym in the Russian literary and political magazine *Sovremennik* ("The Contemporary") in 1852. The story was based on Tolstoy's own memories and was titled *Detstvo* (*Childhood*). More stories and accounts based on his experiences in the Caucasus, including *Nabeg* (1853; "The Raid") and three sketches about the Siege of Sevastopol during the Crimean War, were soon published. Tolstoy was a well-known author by 1856, although his refusal to join any intellectual camp, coupled with his vanity and independence, kept him from being accepted by some from the literary world.

Tolstoy's works during the late 1850s and early '60s experimented with new forms for expressing his moral and philosophical concerns. To *Childhood* Tolstoy soon added *Otrochestvo* (1854; *Boyhood*) and *Yunost* (1857; *Youth*). A number of stories center on a single semiautobiographical character, Dmitry Nekhlyudov, who later reappeared as the hero of Tolstoy's novel *Resurrection* (1899).

In 1862 Tolstoy married Sofya (Sonya) Andreyevna Bers and soon transferred all his energies to his marriage and to the composition of the historical novel *Voyna i mir* (*War and Peace*). One of Tolstoy's best-known works, *War and Peace* is an epic novel of Russian life during the time of French emperor Napoleon. It was completed in 1869. The work contains three kinds of material—a historical account of the Napoleonic wars, the biographies of fictional characters, and a set of essays about the philosophy of history. Equally successful was Tolstoy's novel *Anna Karenina* (1875–77), a psychological study of 19th-century Russian social life. In it Tolstoy interweaves the stories of three families while focusing on the tragic character of Anna. Through Anna's story Tolstoy indicates that the romantic idea of love, which most people identify with love itself, is entirely incompatible with the superior kind of love—the intimate love of good families.

After 1879 Tolstoy changed his way of life. He determined to live by a code of nonviolence, universal love and forgiveness, and simplicity. This moral crisis was recorded in his *Ispoved* (1884; *My Confession*). His subsequent nonfiction writings became increasingly devoted to his beliefs. Two of them were *Tsarstvo bozhiye vnutri vas* (1893; *The Kingdom of God Is Within You*) and *Chto takoye iskusstvo?* (1898; *What Is Art?*). Tolstoy's creed attracted many followers, who were called Tolstoyans.

Tolstoy's later fiction was divided into two groups. First, he wrote a number of moral tales for common people, including "Gde lyubov, tam i bog" (written 1885; "Where Love Is, God Is") and "Mnogo li cheloveku zemli nuzhno" (written 1885; "How Much Land Does a Man Need"). Second, he wrote realistic fiction for educated people. The latter category included *Smert Ivana Ilicha* (written 1886; *The Death of Ivan Ilyich*), a novella describing a man's gradual realization that he is dying and that his life has been wasted on trivialities, and *Otets Sergy* (written 1898; *Father Sergius*), which tells the story of a proud man who wants to become a saint but discovers that sainthood cannot be consciously sought.

Tolstoy was often in opposition to the Russian government and the church. Many of his works were censored, and his followers were persecuted. Tolstoy, however, was protected from harm by his worldwide fame and by the love the Russian people had for him.

Tolstoy and his family were driven apart by conflicts in their beliefs. At the age of 82 he left the family estate at Yasnaya Polyana, intending never to return. Within a few days of his departure, Tolstoy contracted pneumonia and died of heart failure on November 20 (November 7 according to the old calendar), 1910, at the railroad station of Astapovo in the Russian province of Ryazan.

## MARK TWAIN

(b. 1835—d. 1910)

A onetime printer and Mississippi River boat pilot, Mark Twain became one of America's greatest authors. His *Tom Sawyer, Huckleberry Finn*, and *Life on the Mississippi* rank high on any list of great American books.

The sixth child, Mark Twain was born Samuel Langhorne Clemens on November 30, 1835, in the small town of Florida, Missouri. His father was a hard worker but a poor provider. The family moved to Hannibal, Missouri, on the Mississippi, when young Clemens was four years old. It was in this river town that he grew up, and from it he gathered the material for his most famous stories. The character of Judge Carpenter is somewhat like his father; Aunt Polly, his mother; Sid Sawyer, his brother Henry; Huck Finn, a town boy named Tom Blankenship; and Tom Sawyer, a combination of several boys—including himself.

His father died when he was 12, and the boy was apprenticed to a printer. An apprentice works for someone in order to learn a trade. This was the first step toward his career as a writer. In 1857 he apprenticed himself to a riverboat pilot. He became a licensed pilot and spent two and a half years at his new trade. The river swarmed with traffic, and the pilot was the most important man aboard the boat. He wrote of these years in *Life on the Mississippi*.

The Civil War ended his career as a pilot. Clemens went west to Nevada and soon became a reporter on the Virginia City newspaper. Here he began using the pen name Mark Twain. It is an old river term meaning two fathoms, or 12 feet (4 meters), of water depth.

In 1864 he went to California. The next year he wrote his "Jumping Frog" story, which ran in many newspapers. He was sent to the Sandwich

Islands (now Hawaii) as a roving reporter, and on his return he began lecturing. He was soon on a tour of the Mediterranean and the Holy Land. From this came *The Innocents Abroad*, which made him famous.

In 1870 he married Olivia Langdon. She modified Twain's exaggerations, sometimes weakening his writings, sometimes actually making them more readable. Twain began turning out a new book every few years. William Dean Howells, editor of the *Atlantic Monthly* and a highly respected novelist, became his close friend and literary adviser.

Twain bought a publishing firm in Hartford, Connecticut. He earned much money writing, lecturing, and in his publishing house, but he spent it on high living and unsuccessful investments. He lost a fortune promoting a typesetting machine. By 1894 his publishing company had failed and he was bankrupt.

Twain set out on a world lecture tour to retrieve his fortune, and by 1898 his debts were paid. In his last years he traveled and spoke much but wrote comparatively little. He died on April 21, 1910.

Twain was more than a humorist. Behind his mask of humor lay a serious view of life. Tragedy had entered his own life in the poverty and early death of his father, the loss of a daughter, and his bankruptcy. His short story, "The Man That Corrupted Hadleyburg," published in 1900, which showed greed at work in a small town, is an indication of Twain's dark side.

The controversial *Huckleberry Finn*, which is periodically banned in schools or libraries because of alleged racial overtones, can be read by children, but it is not a child's book. It has elements of heartbreak and wisdom that can be appreciated best by adults. On the other hand, *Tom Sawyer* is primarily a juvenile book but one that can be read with pleasure by adults.

Twain's chief works are:*The Celebrated Jumping Frog of Calaveras County*, a collection published in 1867; *The Innocents Abroad* (1869); *Roughing It* (1872); *The Gilded Age—with Charles Dudley Warner* (1873); *The Adventures of Tom Sawyer* (1876); *A Tramp Abroad* (1880); *The Prince and the Pauper* (1882); *Life on the Mississippi* (1883); *The Adventures of Huckleberry Finn* (1884); *A Connecticut Yankee in King Arthur's Court* (1889); *The Tragedy of Pudd'nhead Wilson* (1894); and *Personal Recollections of Joan of Arc* (1896). Printed posthumously were: *The Mysterious Stranger* (1916); *Mark Twain's Notebook* (1935); and *Autobiography* (2010– ).

# MARIO VARGAS LLOSA

(b. 1936—d. )

The novels, plays, and essays of Peruvian writer Mario Vargas Llosa reflect his commitment to social change. In 1990 he was an unsuccessful candidate for president of Peru. Vargas Llosa was awarded the 2010 Nobel Prize in Literature "for his cartography of structures of power and his trenchant images of the individual's resistance, revolt, and defeat."

Jorge Mario Pedro Vargas Llosa was born on March 28, 1936, in Arequipa, Peru. He received his early education in Cochabamba, Bolivia, where his grandfather was the Peruvian consul. Vargas Llosa later attended a series of schools in Peru before entering a military school, Leoncio Prado, in Lima in 1950.

After Vargas Llosa's first publication, *La huida del Inca* (1952; *The Escape of the Inca*), a three-act play, his stories began to appear in Peruvian literary reviews. He coedited the reviews *Cuadernos de composición* (Composition Book) in 1956–57 and Literatura in 1958–59. He also worked as a journalist and broadcaster and attended the University of Madrid. In 1959 he moved to Paris, where he lived until 1966. He later lived in England, the United States, and Spain before returning to Lima in 1974.

Vargas Llosa's first novel, *La ciudad y los perros* (1963; *The Time of the Hero*), was widely acclaimed. Translated into more than a dozen languages, it describes adolescents striving for survival in the hostile and violent environment of a military school. *La casa verde* (1966; *The Green House*), set in the Peruvian jungle, combines mythical, popular, and heroic elements to capture the tragic and fragmented reality of its characters. *Conversación en La Catedral* (1969; *Conversation in the Cathedral*) deals with Manuel Odría's military regime (1948–56), and *Pantaleón y las visitadoras* (1973; *Captain Pantoja and the Special Service*) is a satire of military and religious fanaticism. His semiautobiographical novel *La tía Julia y el escribidor* (1977; *Aunt Julia and the Scriptwriter*) combines two narrative points of view to explore the creative process of writing and its relation to the daily lives of writers.

Vargas Llosa also wrote several acclaimed works of criticism, including *García Márquez: Historia de un deicidio* (1971; *García Márquez: Story of a God-Killer*), *La orgía perpetua: Flaubert y "Madame Bovary"* (1975; *The Perpetual Orgy: Flaubert and "Madame Bovary"*), and *Entre Sartre y Camus* (1981; Between Sartre and Camus). A collection of his critical essays was published in English translation in 1978.

Mario Vargas Llosa, c. 1990.

In 1981 Vargas Llosa published *La guerra del fin del mundo* (*The War of the End of the World*), an account of a 19th-century Brazilian apocalyptic religious movement; it became a best-seller in Spanish-speaking countries. His later works include the plays *La Señorita de Tacna* (1981; *The Lady of Tacna*) and *La Chunga* (1986; *The Jest*) and the novels *El hablador* (1987; *The Storyteller*) and *Lituma en los Andes* (1993; *Death in the Andes*).

Although often considered antipolitical, Vargas Llosa challenged Alberto Fujimori for the presidency of Peru in 1990. He lost the election in a runoff. In 1994 he won the Cervantes prize, the Spanish-speaking world's highest literary award.

## JULES VERNE

(b. 1828—d. 1905)

The startling inventions described in the novels of Jules Verne seemed highly fantastic to the readers of his time. Today he is regarded as a prophet. His dreams of undersea and air travel have come true, and Verne's story *Around the World in Eighty Days* now seems a record of a leisurely trip.

Jules Verne was born on February 8, 1828, in Nantes, France. With his brother, young Jules sailed on the Loire River, often going down to the sea. To the boy's active imagination the leaky boat was a palatial yacht and every scene an important geographic discovery. His father was a lawyer and wanted Jules to follow the same profession. When Jules was sent to school in Paris, however, he studied literature instead of law.

Verne began to write poetry and plays at an early age, but he had little success until he published *Five Weeks in a Balloon* in 1863. This fantastic tale delighted readers, both young and old. Its success led Verne to continue writing exciting stories of adventure. He studied geography and science to get ideas for his tales.

Verne's works include many short stories and more than 50 novels. The most popular novels include *A Journey to the Center of the Earth* (1864); *From the Earth to the Moon* (1865); *The Mysterious Island* (1870); *Twenty Thousand Leagues Under the Sea* (1870); and *Around the World in Eighty Days* (1872).

## KURT VONNEGUT, JR.

(b. 1922—d. 2007)

Characterized by grim humor and a preoccupation with the hostile forces of science and technology, Kurt Vonnegut, Jr., has written numerous novels in which he pleads for human kindness in the present world and in the dehumanized world he depicts as the future.

Vonnegut was born on November 11, 1922, in Indianapolis, Indiana. He attended Cornell University before serving in the United States Air Force in World War II. As a German prisoner of war, Vonnegut was a survivor of the fire bombing of Dresden, Germany, in February 1945. After the war Vonnegut studied anthropology at the University of Chicago and worked as a police reporter and a public relations writer before leaving to write full-time.

Kurt Vonnegut, Jr.

Vonnegut began his writing career with short stories for magazines. His first novel, *Player Piano*, was published in 1952, followed by *The Sirens of Titan* (1959), *Mother Night* (1961), and *God Bless You, Mr. Rosewater* (1965). Vonnegut gained attention from the critics and the reading public with *Cat's Cradle* (1963). His best-known work, *Slaughterhouse-Five*, or *The Children's Crusade* (1969), is an autobiographical but fictional recreation of the Dresden bombing as experienced by a naive American soldier, Billy Pilgrim, imprisoned in a meat storage cellar below a slaughterhouse.

Later novels include *Breakfast of Champions* (1973), *Slapstick* (1976), *Jailbird* (1979), *Deadeye Dick* (1982), *Galápagos* (1985), *Bluebeard* (1987), *Hocus Pocus* (1990), and *Timequake* (1997). Vonnegut also wrote the play *Happy Birthday, Wanda June* (1970), the collection of short stories *Welcome to the Monkey House* (1968), and the nonfiction works *Wampeters, Foma & Grandfalloons* (1974), *Palm Sunday* (1981), and *A Man Without a Country* (2005). Vonnegut died on April 11, 2007, in New York, New York.

## ALICE WALKER

(b. 1944—d. )

Alice Malsenior Walker is an American writer whose novels, short stories, and poems are noted for their insightful treatment of African American culture. Her novels, most notably *The Color Purple* (1982), focus particularly on women.

Walker was the eighth child of African American sharecroppers. While growing up she was accidentally blinded in one eye, and her mother gave her a typewriter, allowing her to write instead of doing chores. She received a scholarship to attend Spelman College, where she studied for two years before transferring to Sarah Lawrence College. After graduating in 1965, Walker moved to Mississippi and became involved in the civil rights movement. She also began teaching and publishing short stories and essays. She married in 1967, but the couple divorced in 1976.

Walker's first book of poetry, *Once*, appeared in 1968, and her first novel, *The Third Life of Grange Copeland* (1970), a narrative that spans 60

Alice Walker.

years and three generations, followed two years later. A second volume of poetry, *Revolutionary Petunias and Other Poems*, and her first collection of short stories, *In Love and Trouble: Stories of Black Woman*, both appeared in 1973. The latter bears witness to sexist violence and abuse in the African American community. After moving to New York, Walker completed *Meridian* (1976), a novel describing the coming of age of several civil rights workers in the 1960s.

Walker later moved to California, where she wrote her most popular novel, *The Color Purple* (1982). An epistolary novel, it depicts the growing up and self-realization of an African American woman between 1909 and 1947 in a town in Georgia. The book won a Pulitzer Prize and was adapted into a film by Steven Spielberg in 1985. A musical version produced by Oprah Winfrey and Quincy Jones premiered in 2004.

Walker's later fiction includes *The Temple of My Familiar*, an ambitious examination of racial and sexual tensions (1989); *Possessing the Secret of Joy* (1992), a narrative centred on female genital mutilation; *By the Light of My Father's Smile* (1998), the story of a family of anthropologists posing as missionaries in order to gain access to a Mexican tribe; and *Now Is the Time to Open Your Heart* (2005), about an older woman's quest for identity. Reviewers complained that these novels employed New Age abstractions and poorly conceived characters, though Walker continued to draw praise for championing racial and gender equality in her work. She also released the volume of short stories *The Way Forward Is with a Broken Heart* (2000) and several other volumes of poetry, including *Absolute Trust in the Goodness of the Earth* (2003) and *A Poem Traveled Down My Arm* (2003). *Her Blue Body Everything We Know: Earthling Poems* (1991) collects poetry from 1965 to 1990.

Her essays were compiled in *In Search of Our Mother's Gardens: Womanist Prose* (1983), *Sent by Earth: A Message from the Grandmother Spirit After the Bombing of the World Trade Center and Pentagon* (2001), *We Are the Ones We Have Been Waiting For* (2006), and *The Cushion in the Road: Meditation and Wandering as the Whole World Awakens to Being in Harm's Way* (2013). Walker also wrote juvenile fiction and critical essays on such female writers as Flannery O'Connor and Zora Neale Hurston. She cofounded a short-lived press in 1984.

# EDITH WHARTON

(b. 1862—d. 1937)

The upper-class society into which Edith Wharton was born provided her with abundant material for plotting her novels and short stories. Her major literary model was Henry James, a close friend in her later years. Like him, she lived a great part of her life in Europe, rarely returning to the United States after 1907.

Edith Wharton.

Wharton was born Edith Newbold Jones in New York City on January 24, 1862. She was educated by private tutors at home and in Europe. She married Boston banker Edward Wharton in 1885. Her first novel, *The Valley of Decision*, was published in 1902. Critical acclaim came with *The House of Mirth* in 1905. It analyzed the aristocratic society she knew and its reaction to social change.

A similar theme was evident in *The Custom of the Country* (1913), *Twilight Sleep* (1927), *Hudson River Bracketed* (1929), and *The Gods Arrive* (1932). Her most enduring novel was *Ethan Frome* (1911), which explored the grim and often anguished nature of New England farm life. *The Age of Innocence* (1920), which won a Pulitzer Prize, is considered her finest work.

She was divorced from Wharton in 1913. In 1923, on her last visit to the United States, she became the first woman to receive an honorary doctorate from Yale University. In all, she published more than 50 books, including fiction, poetry, travel books, and literary criticism. She died on August 11, 1937, in St-Brice-sous-Forêt, France.

# WALT WHITMAN

(b. 1819—d. 1892)

When they first appeared, Walt Whitman's poems were considered formless, crude, and often immoral. Today many consider Whitman to be the greatest American poet.

Walter Whitman was born in West Hills, Long Island, New York, on May 31, 1819, the second of six children. His father was a carpenter. Young Whitman tried many jobs. He was an office boy, printer, schoolteacher, reporter, and for a time the editor of the *Brooklyn Eagle* and other newspapers. At 30 he took a trip to New Orleans. He saw the vastness of his country for the first time, and he began to set down in poetry his impressions of the nation and its people.

No publisher or author's name was on the first edition of *Leaves of Grass* in 1855. Whitman printed it himself, and throughout his life he continued to publish expansions and revisions of the work. He sent copies of the first edition to well-known literary men. Some condemned the book, but Ralph Waldo Emerson saw its merit. In the 1856 edition Whitman printed Emerson's letter of praise, which called the book "the most extraordinary piece of wit and wisdom yet contributed to American literature."

Early in the American Civil War Whitman learned that his brother

George was wounded and in a hospital in Washington, D.C. He found George nearly recovered but saw other soldiers badly in need of care. He stayed in Washington as a government clerk and also served as a hospital volunteer. Inspired by the suffering he saw, he wrote the volume of poetry called *Drum-Taps*, published in 1865.

After the war Whitman's books began to sell well, and he contributed several articles to magazines. In 1873 he fell ill, suffering the first of several paralytic attacks. He remained an invalid for the rest of his life. Choosing Camden, New Jersey, as his last home, he lived modestly, enjoying the visits of those who came to honor him. He died on March 26, 1892.

Among Whitman's other books of poems were *Calamus*, *November Boughs*, *Sands at Seventy*, and *Good-Bye My Fancy*. His prose works include *Democratic Vistas*, *Specimen Days and Collect*, *The Wound Dresser* (wartime letters to his mother), *A Backward Glance O'er Travel'd Roads*, and *Diary in Canada*.

# ELIE WIESEL

(b. 1928—d. )

A prolific writer, teacher, and philosopher, Elie Wiesel was awarded the Nobel Peace Prize in 1986 for his efforts against violence, hatred, and oppression. He was a survivor of the Nazi Holocaust, and his writings and lectures provided a sober, passionate testament to the destruction of European Jewry during World War II.

Eliezer Wiesel was born on September 30, 1928, in Sighet, Romania. When he was 16 his family was deported to the Auschwitz death camp along with all the Jews of Sighet. His parents and sister were killed, but young Wiesel was forced into slave labor at Buchenwald, another German death camp. After the war Wiesel settled in France, where he studied at the Sorbonne and worked as a journalist. In 1956 he moved to the United States, becoming a citizen in 1963. From 1976 he taught at Boston University.

In his first book, *Night*, Wiesel recounts the horrors of his experiences

Elie Wiesel in 2001.

at the hands of the Nazis. Other works—including *The Town Beyond the Wall*, *A Beggar in Jerusalem*, and *The Fifth Son*—reflect the influence of Hasidic tradition, the Talmud, and French existentialism. Wiesel received the Congressional Gold Medal and the Presidential Medal of Freedom and was named a commander in the French Legion of Honor.

## OSCAR WILDE

(b. 1854—d. 1900)

The Irish poet and dramatist Oscar Wilde wrote some of the finest comedies in the English language: *Lady Windermere's Fan*, published in 1892, *A Woman of No Importance* (1893), *An Ideal Husband* (1895), and the ever-popular *The Importance of Being Earnest* (1895). He was a great conversationalist and a man of wide learning, but his life ended in disgrace and poverty.

Wilde was born on October 16, 1854, in Dublin, Ireland. He was educated at Portora Royal School in Enniskillen, Trinity College in Dublin, and Magdalen College, Oxford. He then settled in London, where in 1884 he married Constance Lloyd. They had two sons. He published his early poetry, wrote book reviews, and edited the journal *Woman's World*. His only novel, *The Picture of Dorian Gray* (1891), was severely criticized as immoral. He had the ability to take conventional plots and turn them into brilliant comedies by his witty dialogue. In the classic *The Importance of Being Earnest*, the plot and the dialogue are equally fantastic.

In 1891 Wilde began an ill-fated friendship with Lord Alfred Douglas, whose father objected violently to Wilde. Wilde sued the father for libel. The case collapsed, and Wilde himself was arrested for homosexual offenses under the Criminal Law Amendment Act of 1895. Wilde was found guilty and sentenced on May 25, 1895, to two years at hard labor. He recounted his prison experience in *The Ballad of Reading Gaol* (1898). After his release he left England, never to return. He divided his time between France and Italy, living in comparative poverty. But he continued to delight a small circle of friends with his conversation. Except for letters, he made no attempt to resume writing. He died in Paris on November 30, 1900.

# TENNESSEE WILLIAMS

(b. 1911—d. 1983)

The dramas of Tennessee Williams are some of the most moving and powerful ever written for the American stage. His Southern settings and characters depict a world of human frustration in which sex and violence underlie an atmosphere of superficial, faded gentility.

He was born Thomas Lanier Williams on March 26, 1911, in Columbus, Mississippi. He attended the University of Missouri from 1931 to 1933 and Washington University in St. Louis (1936–37), where he became interested in writing. Williams worked at it during the Great Depression while employed in a shoe factory. He studied dramatic writing at the University of Iowa, from which he graduated in 1938. Afterward he traveled around the country, working at insignificant jobs and writing short plays that were often produced at community theaters. He won some recognition for *American Blues* (1939), a group of one-act plays.

Williams continued doing odd jobs, however, until his first real success in 1944: *The Glass Menagerie*, a play about a decadent Southern family living under great emotional tension in a city tenement. The play won the New York Drama Critic's Circle award, as did three more of his plays. His next major play was *A Streetcar Named Desire* (1947), a study of the mental and moral ruin of a former Southern belle, Blanche Du Bois. Her genteel pretensions are no match for her brutish brother-in-law, Stanley Kowalski. This success was followed by *Camino Real* (1953), *Cat on a Hot Tin Roof* (1955), *Suddenly Last Summer* (1958), *Sweet Bird of Youth* (1959), and *Night of the Iguana* (1961). *A Streetcar Named Desire* and *Cat on a Hot Tin Roof* were both awarded Pulitzer Prizes. In addition to long theater runs, all of these plays were filmed. His novel *The Roman Spring of Mrs. Stone* (1950) also became a motion picture.

Williams's later writing was compromised by health problems, addiction to alcohol and sleeping pills, and a nervous breakdown. His last plays were not well received. He died in New York City on February 25, 1983.

## MARY WOLLSTONECRAFT

(b. 1759—d. 1797)

English writer and women's rights advocate Mary Wollstonecraft argued for female political, economic, and legal equality. In her most important work, *A Vindication of the Rights of Woman* (1792), she calls for women and men to be educated equally.

Wollstonecraft was born on April 27, 1759, in London. She taught school and worked as a governess, jobs that helped form the views put forth in her *Thoughts on the Education of Daughters* (1787). In 1788 she became a translator for the London publisher James Johnson. There she published several of her works, including the novel *Mary: A Fiction* (1788). A few years later her work on woman's place in society, *A Vindication of the Rights of Woman*, came out. In it she argues that educating girls to the same degree as boys would result in women who would be not only exceptional wives and mothers but also capable workers in many professions. The publication of this work caused considerable controversy but did not bring about any immediate reforms. Beginning in the 1840s, however, members of the American and European women's movements, including U.S. women's rights pioneers Elizabeth Cady Stanton and Margaret Fuller, popularized some of the book's principles.

Wollstonecraft left England for Paris in 1792 to experience the French Revolution. There she lived with an American, Captain Gilbert Imlay, and in the spring of 1794 she gave birth to a daughter, Fanny. The following year, distraught that her relationship with Imlay had ended, she attempted suicide. Wollstonecraft subsequently returned to London to resume her work for Johnson. She also joined an influential radical group that included William Godwin, Thomas Paine, Thomas Holcroft, William Blake, and William Wordsworth. In 1796 she began an affair with Godwin and became pregnant, and on March 29, 1797, the two were married. The marriage was happy but brief; Wollstonecraft Godwin died in London on September 10, 1797, 11 days after giving birth to her second daughter, Mary. Mary would eventually become the wife of poet Percy Bysshe Shelley and write the gothic novel *Frankenstein*.

# VIRGINIA WOOLF

(b. 1882—d. 1941)

Virginia Woolf was born Virginia Stephen in London on January 25, 1882, and was educated by her father, Sir Leslie Stephen. After his death she set up housekeeping in Gordon Square in the district of Bloomsbury in London. Beginning in about 1907 her home was frequently visited by the young intellectuals who later became known as the Bloomsbury group. Among the group's members were economist John Maynard Keynes, biographer Lytton Strachey, novelist E.M. Forster, and political writer Leonard Woolf. Woolf became her husband in 1912. The couple founded Hogarth Press as a publisher for her own and other authors' books.

Virginia Woolf.

Her first novels—*The Voyage Out*, published in 1915, and *Night and Day* (1919)—were praised by the critics, but she was dissatisfied with them and began to experiment with stream-of-consciousness writing. This is a narrative technique in which the reader lives within the mind of the characters and watches the story unfold. Her first such work was

*Jacob's Room* (1922), followed by *Mrs. Dalloway* (1925), *To the Lighthouse* (1927), and *The Waves* (1931). *Between the Acts* (1941) was her last novel.

Virginia Woolf was plagued by emotional problems for many years. During a period of disturbance she drowned herself in Sussex on March 28, 1941. In the decades after her death, her long essay, *A Room of One's Own* (1929), became a major text of the feminist movement. In it she describes the difficulties encountered by women writers in a society dominated by males.

## RICHARD WRIGHT

(b. 1908—d. 1960)

The American author Richard Wright pictured with brutal realism what it meant to be black in a white society. His writings speak with the raw voice of an anguish not often evident in novels.

Richard Nathaniel Wright was born on September 4, 1908, on a plantation near Natchez, Mississippi. His father was a mill hand, and his mother taught in a country school. Young Wright's childhood was generally one of poverty, frustration, and despair. When he was 5 his father left the family, and when he was not yet 10, his mother became paralyzed. He was sent to live with relatives. At 15 he left home and for several years drifted from one city to another, working at whatever jobs he could find. In Chicago he worked nights in the post office. Days he spent reading and writing. During the depression of the 1930s, he lost his job and had to go on relief. Not long afterward he joined the Communist party, as did thousands of other young Americans at the time.

In 1937 Wright moved to New York City, where he worked on a Federal Writers' Project. His first published book, *Uncle Tom's Children*, appeared in 1938. It was a collection of four stories dealing with racial prejudice and violence in the South. But it was Wright's novel *Native Son* (1940) that brought him world fame. This powerful story of a Chicago black driven to crime was made into a play by Wright and Paul Green. It was successfully staged in 1941.

Wright's first marriage—to a ballet dancer—ended in divorce. In 1941 he married Ellen Poplar of New York City, and they had two daughters. Wright became increasingly disillusioned with the Communist party and finally left it. In 1945 he published *Black Boy*, an autobiography of his childhood and youth. It confirmed him as a major American writer.

His discontent with American society persisted. As a youth he had experienced not only hardship but vicious racial prejudice as well, and as a man he continued to encounter it. In 1946 he and his white wife left the United States to live in Paris.

Wright wrote several novels during the next 14 years, but they were not well received. He also wrote some travel books and other nonfiction. On November 28, 1960, he died in Paris of a heart attack.

# WILLIAM BUTLER YEATS

(b. 1865—d. 1939)

Irish poet, dramatist, and prose writer, William Butler Yeats was one of the greatest English-language poets of the 20th century. He received the Nobel Prize in Literature in 1923.

Yeats's father, John Butler Yeats, was a barrister who eventually became a portrait painter. His mother, formerly Susan Pollexfen, was the daughter of a prosperous merchant in Sligo, in western Ireland. Through both parents Yeats claimed kinship with various Anglo-Irish Protestant families who are mentioned in his work. Normally, Yeats would have been expected to identify with his Protestant tradition—which represented a powerful minority among Ireland's predominantly Roman Catholic population—but he did not. Indeed, he was separated from both historical traditions available to him in Ireland—from the Roman Catholics, because he could not share their faith, and from the Protestants, because he felt repelled by their concern for material success. Yeats's best hope, he felt, was to cultivate a tradition more profound than either the Catholic or the Protestant—the tradition of a hidden Ireland that existed largely in the anthropological evidence of its surviving customs, beliefs, and holy places, more pagan than Christian.

In 1867, when Yeats was only two, his family moved to London, but he spent much of his boyhood and school holidays in Sligo with his grandparents. This country—its scenery, folklore, and supernatural legend—would color Yeats's work and form the setting of many of his poems. In 1880 his family moved back to Dublin, where he attended the high school. In 1883 he attended the Metropolitan School of Art in Dublin, where the most important part of his education was in meeting other poets and artists.

Meanwhile, Yeats was beginning to write: his first publication, two brief lyrics, appeared in the *Dublin University Review* in 1885. When the family moved back to London in 1887, Yeats took up the life of a professional writer. He joined the Theosophical Society, whose mysticism appealed to him because it was a form of imaginative life far removed from the workaday world. The age of science was repellent to Yeats; he was a visionary, and he insisted upon surrounding himself with poetic images. He began a study of the prophetic books of William Blake, and this enterprise brought him into contact with other visionary traditions, such as the Platonic, the Neoplatonic, the Swedenborgian, and the alchemical.

Yeats was already a proud young man, and his pride required him to rely on his own taste and his sense of artistic style. He was not boastful, but spiritual arrogance came easily to him. His early poems, collected in *The Wanderings of Oisin, and Other Poems* (1889), are the work of an aesthete, often beautiful but always rarefied, a soul's cry for release from circumstance.

Yeats quickly became involved in the literary life of London. He became friends with William Morris and W.E. Henley, and he was a cofounder of the Rhymers' Club, whose members included his friends Lionel Johnson and Arthur Symons. In 1889 Yeats met Maud Gonne, an Irish beauty, ardent and brilliant. From that moment, as he wrote, "the troubling of my life began." He fell in love with her, but his love was hopeless. Maud Gonne liked and admired him, but she was not in love with him. Her passion was lavished upon Ireland; she was an Irish patriot, a rebel, and a rhetorician, commanding in voice and in person. When Yeats joined in the Irish nationalist cause, he did so partly from conviction, but mostly for love of Maud. When Yeats's play *Cathleen ni Houlihan* was first performed in Dublin in 1902, she played the title role. It was during this period that Yeats came under the influence of John O'Leary, a charismatic leader of the Fenians, a secret society of Irish nationalists.

After the rapid decline and death of the controversial Irish leader Charles Stewart Parnell in 1891, Yeats felt that Irish political life lost its significance. The vacuum left by politics might be filled, he felt, by literature, art, poetry, drama, and legend. *The Celtic Twilight* (1893), a volume of essays, was Yeats's first effort toward this end, but progress was slow until 1898, when he met Augusta Lady Gregory, an aristocrat who was to become a playwright and his close friend. She was already collecting old stories, the lore of the west of Ireland. Yeats found that this lore chimed with his feeling for ancient ritual, for pagan beliefs never entirely destroyed by Christianity. He felt that if he could treat it in a strict and high style, he would create a genuine poetry while, in personal terms, moving toward his own identity. From 1898, Yeats spent his summers at Lady Gregory's home, Coole Park, County Galway, and he eventually purchased a ruined Norman castle called Thoor Ballylee in the neighbourhood. Under the name of the Tower, this structure would become a dominant symbol in many of his latest and best poems.

In 1899 Yeats asked Maud Gonne to marry him, but she declined. Four years later she married Major John MacBride, an Irish soldier who shared her feeling for Ireland and her hatred of English oppression: he was one of the rebels later executed by the British government for their part in the Easter Rising of 1916. Meanwhile, Yeats devoted himself to literature and drama, believing that poems and plays would engender a national unity capable of transfiguring the Irish nation. He (along with Lady Gregory and others) was one of the originators of the Irish Literary Theatre, which gave its first performance in Dublin in 1899 with Yeats's play *The Countess Cathleen*. To the end of his life Yeats remained a director of this theatre, which became the Abbey Theatre in 1904. In the crucial period from 1899 to 1907, he managed the theatre's affairs, encouraged its playwrights (notably John Millington Synge), and contributed many of his own plays. Among the latter that became part of the Abbey Theatre's repertoire are *The Land of Heart's Desire* (1894), *Cathleen ni Houlihan* (1902), *The Hour Glass* (1903), *The King's Threshold* (1904), *On Baile's Strand* (1905), and *Deirdre* (1907).

Yeats published several volumes of poetry during this period, notably

*Poems* (1895) and *The Wind Among the Reeds* (1899), which are typical of his early verse in their dreamlike atmosphere and their use of Irish folklore and legend. But in the collections *In the Seven Woods* (1903) and *The Green Helmet* (1910), Yeats slowly discarded the Pre-Raphaelite colours and rhythms of his early verse and purged it of certain Celtic and esoteric influences. The years from 1909 to 1914 mark a decisive change in his poetry. The otherworldly, ecstatic atmosphere of the early lyrics has cleared, and the poems in *Responsibilities: Poems and a Play* (1914) show a tightening and hardening of his verse line, a more sparse and resonant imagery, and a new directness with which Yeats confronts reality and its imperfections.

In 1917 Yeats published *The Wild Swans at Coole*. From then onward he reached and maintained the height of his achievement—a renewal of inspiration and a perfecting of technique that are almost without parallel in the history of English poetry. *The Tower* (1928), named after the castle he owned and had restored, is the work of a fully accomplished artist; in it, the experience of a lifetime is brought to perfection of form. Still, some of Yeats's greatest verse was written subsequently, appearing in *The Winding Stair* (1929). The poems in both of these works use, as their dominant subjects and symbols, the Easter Rising and the Irish civil war; Yeats's own tower; the Byzantine Empire and its mosaics; Plato, Plotinus, and Porphyry; and the author's interest in contemporary psychical research. Yeats explained his own philosophy in the prose work *A Vision* (1925, revised version 1937); this meditation upon the relation between imagination, history, and the occult remains indispensable to serious students of Yeats despite its obscurities.

In 1913 Yeats spent some months at Stone Cottage, Sussex, with the American poet Ezra Pound acting as his secretary. Pound was then editing translations of the nō plays of Japan, and Yeats was greatly excited by them. The *nō* drama provided a framework of drama designed for a small audience of initiates, a stylized, intimate drama capable of fully using the resources offered by masks, mime, dance, and song and conveying—in contrast to the public theatre—Yeats's own recondite symbolism. Yeats devised what he considered an equivalent of the *nō* drama in such plays as *Four Plays for Dancers* (1921), *At the Hawk's Well* (first performed 1916), and several others.

In 1917 Yeats asked Iseult Gonne, Maud Gonne's daughter, to marry him. She refused. Some weeks later he proposed to Miss George Hyde-Lees and was accepted; they were married in 1917. A daughter, Anne Butler Yeats, was born in 1919, and a son, William Michael Yeats, in 1921.

In 1922, on the foundation of the Irish Free State, Yeats accepted an invitation to become a member of the new Irish Senate: he served for six years. In 1923 he was awarded the Nobel Prize in Literature. Now a celebrated figure, he was indisputably one of the most significant modern poets. In 1936 his *Oxford Book of Modern Verse*, 1892–1935, a gathering of the poems he loved, was published. Still working on his last plays, he completed *The Herne's Egg*, his most raucous work, in 1938. Yeats's last two verse collections, *New Poems* and *Last Poems and Two Plays*, appeared in 1938 and 1939 respectively. In these books many of his previous themes are gathered up and rehandled, with an immense technical range; the aged poet was using ballad rhythms and dialogue structure with undiminished energy as he approached his 75th year.

Yeats died in January 1939 while abroad. Final arrangements for his burial in Ireland could not be made, so he was buried at Roquebrune, France. The intention of having his body buried in Sligo was thwarted when World War II began in the autumn of 1939. In 1948 his body was finally taken back to Sligo and buried in a little Protestant churchyard at Drumcliffe, as he specified in "Under Ben Bulben," in his *Last Poems*, under his own epitaph: "Cast a cold eye/On life, on death./Horseman, pass by!"

Had Yeats ceased to write at age 40, he would probably now be valued as a minor poet writing in a dying Pre-Raphaelite tradition that had drawn renewed beauty and poignancy for a time from the Celtic revival. There is no precedent in literary history for a poet who produces his greatest work between the ages of 50 and 75. Yeats's work of this period takes its strength from his long and dedicated apprenticeship to poetry; from his experiments in a wide range of forms of poetry, drama, and prose; and from his spiritual growth and his gradual acquisition of personal wisdom, which he incorporated into the framework of his own mythology.

Yeats's mythology, from which arises the distilled symbolism of his great period, is not always easy to understand, nor did Yeats intend its full meaning to be immediately apparent to those unfamiliar with his thought and the tradition in which he worked. His own cyclic view of history suggested to him a recurrence and convergence of images, so that they become multiplied and enriched; and this progressive enrichment may be traced throughout his work. Among Yeats's dominant images are Leda and the Swan; Helen and the burning of Troy; the Tower in its many forms; the sun and moon; the burning house; cave, thorn tree, and well; eagle, heron, sea gull, and hawk; blind man, lame man, and beggar; unicorn and phoenix; and horse, hound, and boar. Yet these traditional images are continually validated by their alignment with Yeats's own personal experience, and it is this that gives them their peculiarly vital quality. In Yeats's verse they are often shaped into a strong and proud rhetoric and into the many poetic tones of which he was the master. All are informed by the two qualities which Yeats valued and which he retained into old age—passion and joy.

# ÉMILE ZOLA

(b. 1840—d. 1902)

As a writer Émile Zola waged two great battles—a long struggle for the acceptance of his powerful novels and the courageous defense of Captain Alfred Dreyfus in the political-military scandal that divided France. Zola won both fights. The critics and the public both realized that his novels were serious studies of mankind, and Dreyfus was eventually exonerated.

Émile-Édouard-Charles-Antoine Zola was born on April 2, 1840, in Paris. His father was an Italian-Greek engineer, his mother a French woman. When young Zola was two the family moved to Aix-en-Provence. His father soon died, and his mother struggled to support the boy. In 1858 Zola returned to Paris. After two years of study at the Lycée St-Louis, he worked at odd jobs and began writing. Zola lived a meager existence for years. But with the publication of *Thérèse Raquin* in 1867, his name became known. Then he launched a series of 20 books known as the Rougon-Macquart novels.

In the series Zola attempted to define men and women as products of heredity and environment. He portrayed them as passive creatures—victims of their own passions and of the circumstances of birth. Like many reformers, he chose extreme examples to prove his points. Whether or not his stories are balanced presentations of life, his writing is full of vivid description and swift-paced narrative.

At the close of his career Zola enjoyed wealth and acclaim, but he could not help taking sides in the most flaming issue of his time—the Dreyfus affair. Dreyfus had been convicted of selling military secrets to the Germans and had been sent to Devil's Island. Zola became convinced that Dreyfus was innocent. To the very great embarrassment of the French authorities, Zola published a document called "J'accuse" ("I Accuse"), which led to his own trial and the reopening of the Dreyfus case. Both men were vindicated completely. Zola died on September 28, 1902, asphyxiated when a faulty chimney in his bedroom became clogged.

With Gustave Flaubert, the Goncourt brothers, and others, Zola helped found the Naturalist school of French literature. Their concentration on misery and misfortune swung public taste away from Romanticism to a middle road of balanced taste. Zola's best-known works are the Rougon-Macquart series (1871–93), including *L'Assommoir* (*The Dramshop*, 1877), *Germinal* (1885), *La Débâcle* (*The Downfall*, 1892), and *Nana* (1880).

# GLOSSARY

**AUTOBIOGRAPHY** A biography written by the person it is about.

**AVANT-GARDE** A group of people who develop new and often very surprising ideas in art and literature.

**CAPITALISM** An economic system characterized by private or corporate ownership of capital goods, by investments that are determined by private decision, and by prices, production, and the distribution of goods that are determined mainly by competition in a free market.

**CAPTIVATE** To attract and hold the attention of someone.

**CHRONICLE** To describe a series of events in the order that they happened.

**CLERGY** People (such as priests) who are the leaders of a religion and who perform religious services.

**CONTROVERSIAL** Relating to or causing much discussion, disagreement, or argument.

**DISILLUSION** To cause (someone) to stop believing that something is good, valuable, or true.

**DYSTOPIA** An imaginary place where people are unhappy and usually afraid because they are not treated fairly.

**ECCENTRIC** Tending to act in strange or unusual ways.

**GENTRY** Upper or ruling class.

**LURID** Causing shock or disgust.

**METAPHOR** A word or phrase for one thing that is used to refer to another thing in order to show or suggest that they are similar.

**NONCONFORMIST** A person who does not behave the way most people behave.

**OUTLANDISH** Extremely different from what is normal or expected.

**PROLIFIC** Producing a large amount of something.

**PROPHETIC** Correctly stating what will happen in the future.

**PSEUDONYM** A name that someone (such as a writer) uses instead of his or her real name.

**REALISM** A style of art or literature that shows or describes people and things as they are in real life.

**RENAISSANCE** The period of European history between the 14th and 17th centuries when there was a new interest in science and in ancient art and literature, especially in Italy.

**SATIRE** A way of using humor to show that someone or something is foolish, weak, or bad.

**SUFFRAGE** The right to vote in an election.

**TEMPERANCE** The practice of always controlling your actions, thoughts, or feelings so that you do not eat or drink too much, become too angry, etc.

**TOTALITARIANISM** The political concept that the citizen should be totally subject to an absolute state authority.

**TRANSCENDENTALISM** A philosophy which says that thought and spiritual things are more real than ordinary human experience and material things.

**ULTRAISM** The principles of those who advocate extreme measures (as radicalism).

# INDEX

## A



## B



## C

# H



# I



# J



# K



# L

## M



## N



## O



## P

## R



## S



## T